By Mike Watt

Enjoy! Mark!
Mike! Watt!

For everyone who supported me all these years, above and beyond reason,

but especially:

My parents, Mary and Bill; my sister, April;

Dan, Mary, Liz and DeeDee;

Amber, Diane and Danielle;

my good friends and partners at *Sirens of Cinema:* Bob Kuiper; Doc Rhonda Baughman, William Wright, and Debbie Rochon;

in no particular order but eternal thanks: Mr. Lloyd Kaufman; Mort Castle; Chris Golden; John Skipp; David and Tara; Mike and Carolyn; Bill and Gwen; John Bulevich for the answer to the problem of *Sittin' 'Round...;*

Romik for that last-minute cover design;

and, as always, my wife and partner, Amy, for absolutely everything.

PHOBOPHOBIA © 2009 Happy Cloud Publications
ISBN is 1441450157 and EAN-13 is 9781441450159.
All Rights Reserved. No part of this book may be reproduced, in whole or in part, by any means including digital without direct permission from the author.

All persons and locations depicted are fictitious. Any similarity to any persons living or dead, or actual locations, is coincidental.

And to All a Good Night appeared in *Nasty Snips.* Copyright © 2000 Mike Watt.
R.E.M. appeared *The Threshhold #3* published by Crossover Press. Copyright © 1999 Mike Watt.
m.p.h. appeared in *Whispers from the Shattered Forum #2* published by Undaunted Press. Copyright © 2000 Mike Watt.
In the Market for Souls originally appeared in *Dreams of Decadence* #11 published by DNA Publications. Copyright © 2002 Mike Watt.
Harry's Nebula was published online in *Spaceways Weekly,* Copyright © 1999 Mike Watt.
Trapdoor was originally published in *The Asylum Vol. 2 – The Violent Ward,* Published by Darktales Publishing, Copyright © 2002 Mike Watt.
Valentine appeared in *Tourniquet Heart,* published by Prime Books, Copyright © 2002 Mike Watt
All other stories appear here for the first time. Copyright © 2009 Mike Watt

Cover designed by Romik Safarian:
www.romiksafarian.com www.thegildedway.com www.areyouontheline.com

Author photo by David Cooper – www.davidcooperphoto.com

Contents

INTRODUCTION BY AMBER BENSON	4
AFTER TWO IN THE OSSUARY	6
AND TO ALL A GOOD NIGHT	13
R.E.M.	14
M.P.H.	22
IN THE MARKET FOR SOULS	30
WAITING FOR THE MAN	45
VALENTINE	56
HARRY'S NEBULA	58
THE SPONGED STONE	67
SCRIMSHAW	83
A ROOF ABOVE OUR HEADS	99
SITTIN 'ROUND FEELIN SORRY	111
TRAPDOR	115
THE NAKED BONES OF AN ECHO	140

Introduction

By Amber Benson

I encountered the institution that is Mike Watt a number of years ago when he interviewed me, I think, for *Film Threat Magazine*.

Knowing Mike and his lovely wife, Amy, it only makes sense that our first in the flesh meeting would occur in the green room of a Science Fiction Convention. Where else do you meet the most fascinating people in the world, but standing around a table full of pre-fab appetizers while vampires, storm troopers and assorted other sci-fi standbys mingle nearby?

In the end, I wasn't at all prepared for just how cool Mike and Amy were. Not only was Mike a writer and journalist in his own right —but together, they were probably the most prolific filmmakers to come out of Pennsylvania...well, ever. They embraced genre filmmaker with a healthy love and respect for the medium; writing, directing and producing the kind of films that mainstream Hollywood just isn't good at making anymore.

There is a twisted skein of darkness running through all of Mike's work that is only made *more* surreal when you actually meet him. Seriously, the guy is probably one of the most positive, creative and dedicated individuals that I have ever meet. You would never guess that underneath that mask of normalcy lies a truly horror-infused artiste.

It's kind of frightening.

So, when Mike sent me his collection of short stories, *Phobophobia,* I wasn't in the least surprised by how good they were. I already knew the man had talent, but it's very rare that you find someone who can excel in so many different mediums at once.

I sat down and read *Phobopobia* in one sitting—I just couldn't put the sucker down. What I love most about this collection is that Mike takes every day, normal scenarios and infuses them with a pinch of fear, making the reader want to turn around just to check that they're alone before embarking on the next story.

I only have one beef with Mike after reading these stories and it goes like this: I now can never look at Santa Claus without flinching and I'm kind of scared to close my eyes and go to sleep because I'm a little nervous my dreams will turn into nightmares.

Thanks, Mike.

After Two in the Ossuary

As a kid, like most kids, I dreamed of the far future, of flying cars and alien species. I feared the shadows in my closet and the noises in the basement. I wrote fantastic stories about galactic warfare and horrible creatures that preyed upon innocent kids.

Gradually, as I grew up, I realized that there were far more terrible things going on *here* and *now*, and that we, as in mankind, were doing them. Suddenly, next week seemed as much a mystery as a hundred years in the future. And the shadows and midnight noises weren't nearly as terrifying as random violence and terrorism.

Older still, and I realized that tomorrow could hold as much dread for me as next week. And "terrorists" were the least of my worries. Criminals in my own neighborhood, striking not only my home, but those of my loved ones—these were suddenly my night terrors. I started to reminisce fondly about the monsters under my bed.

Through all of this maturity of fear, my writing began to change. Of course, this isn't a revelation, or shouldn't be. Every writer goes through a gradual metamorphosis if he sticks with the craft and tries to improve. I'm still evolving—at least I hope I am.

The stories in this collection represent the "middle period" of my career. There were a few things published both before and after these, dealing with the far-flung future and the most horrible of monsters. But those were excluded for a number of reasons from consideration. The primary reasons: a.) They just didn't fit within the context—too far in the future or too fantastic; or b.) They were terrible. (I've developed a theory recently: there are computer viruses that can worm into text files left dormant for long periods of time. These viruses take perfectly serviceable writing—glorious, even—and warp them into terrible prose, nearly unintelligible scribbling. There were stories that I'd actually been *paid for* that were, sometime during the years of last reading and today, somehow twisted and perverted into large piles of literary dung, figuratively speaking. Those were the first to go. *Then* came the "contextual" jettisons.)

The bulk of my so-called "professional writing", hammered out for various print and electronic fiction publications, dealt with the aforementioned "here and now horror". Most of them deal with fantastical elements like monsters or spirits because, well, they're horror stories. But the monsters and spirits are usually the least of the characters' problems. Everything takes place in modern time—*now*, if not necessarily 2008. Because "now" is where most of us live. And it's pretty scary here.

There is one exception in this entire collection, included here simply because I really like it and am really proud of it. It's the one bright and shiny bit of hope amidst the grim and grit. That story is *Harry's Nebula*. It's the solitary piece of science fiction here and it's placed strategically in the middle to break up the angst.

All the other stories deal with humans and human-made problems, even the supernatural ones in nature. It will come as no surprise to either the thinking or feeling people that humans are responsible for the majority of life's horrors and it should come as even less a surprise that the majority of that majority is self-inflicted. To a large degree, the base fears at the heart of these stories are what fueled my nightmares: loss of control over your life due to outside forces, loss of control over your own mind, your past sins manifesting in horrible ways, Bad

Karma and good old fashioned psychopaths. It took a long time, though, to realize that the monsters under my bed had become metaphoric.

Because I like reading about what sparks the creative process, I thought I'd take a quick tour of my past mental processes while writing these stories:

And to All a Good Night. Believe it or not, this was one of the Christmas cards my wife, Amy, and I sent out to family and friends. I actually find it very funny. I would have as a kid, too, because that's the kind of kid I was. And am. It originally appeared in a collection published out of the U.K. called "Nasty Snips".

R.E.M. If this wasn't the first story I'd ever had published, I think it was one of the earliest. But it was far from the first I'd ever written. Dreams fascinate me and I'm always frustrated by attempts to capture them in structures of prose or film or television. Neil Gaiman does it best, of course, as does Joss Whedon. But this was my attempt to write a real dream story utilizing dream logic. And the last act of the story is a nightmare I actually had once. But I always found the idea of someone creeping around inside my head while I slept, manipulating my thoughts, to be a little disturbing.

m.p.h. Until this story much of my writing had either been in the third person or in the voice of a young white male. It's been reprinted twice, once in German, and so far, no one has accused me of being a racist. This is the big fear of your life not being your own, spun on a dime without warning.

In the Market for Souls was the *big sale*. Printed in a national magazine called "Dreams of Decadence" and reprinted in their "best of" trade paperback. I wanted to do something where the classic vampire was neither hissing villain nor tragic romantic hero. If you believe in vampires, chances are you believe that they're just trying to get through their lives the same as we are. But there will always be someone who wants to make a buck off your misfortune.

Waiting for the Man is technically not a horror story. It was born out of my love of tough-guy hard-boiled pulp. But it includes a common theme in my writing: the fear of losing a loved one due to your own terrible decisions and having to live with the consequences. As an aside, I had one editor reject this story because Warren Beatty's movie *Bullworth* had just come out and he thought they were too thematically similar. I don't remember writing any rapping or political messages, though, so I filed that rejection slip under "Huh?"

Valentine was written specifically for a collection called "Tourniquet Heart". I was already married at the time, so it couldn't have been born of a bad breakup. Maybe Amy and I had fought over who had to do the dishes… Don't read into this particular story, though. It was supposed to be funny. Not an allegory.

Harry's Nebula is, to date, one of the few "nice" stories I've ever written and had published. It's about friendship and, really, the fear of losing that friendship and having to face that fear when the time comes. And I know you shouldn't have writers as protagonists but, really, what other profession would Harry have had? Carpenters wouldn't really benefit monetarily from friendships with aliens.

The Sponged Stone, I think, speaks for itself. Ebenezer Scrooge is alive and well and more than a bit sick of the whole thing. This is the second story I've ever completed with the "Jefferson Taz" character, who was not meant to be a poor man's John Constantine. I wanted him to be a happy-go-lucky Philip Marlowe who lived with the knowledge that monsters and demons existed and, in general, was okay with that. This is the lightest of the three "Taz" stories here. It's also the lightest of every "Taz" story ever planned. He's been rattling around in my head for a long time.

Scrimshaw is a nasty, vicious thing; a snarling, angry beast of a story. Rape, revenge, poetic justice—it's all here. I've had editors recoil from this story. I got at least three angry rejection slips in response to this story. Sometimes it's nice to get that kind of reaction. You may not have a check at the end of the day, but at least you got your point across.

A Roof Above Our Heads is our next "Taz" story and the last one written to date. It is also the last short story I have written to date. After completing this, other interests and priorities took over my time. But I still have a fondness for it, so here it is.

Sittin' 'Round, Feelin' Sorry on a Lost and Lonely Day. Once upon a time, a publisher solicited for a planned collection of what he was calling "Goth horror". There were no specific guidelines, just the capsulation of the "Goth" lifestyle. Maybe my worldview was too narrow at the time, but to me, the "Goths" I saw at clubs seemed to be moody little bastards who knew how to dress but little else. The "Goths" I knew personally were whiny pessimists I called "Oh My Goths" and are now, as I understand, referred to as "Emo". Maybe this is an unfair characteristic, but that's where the story came from. As it turns out, this wasn't what the publisher was looking for. A few months later, the project was cancelled, which made me think, "How appropriately Goth."

Trapdoor is the second-most reprinted story of my short career, in a couple of different languages. It came from a nightmare I had when I was sick with the flu. More than anything else, this is the story focusing on the fear of losing your mind, of hating who you are and hating who you might be more. It also, to me, perfectly sums up male insecurity.

The Naked Bones of an Echo. Might as well end with a novella. This was the first completed Jefferson Taz story. Before this, he'd been living in a lot of outlines, biding his time until I got around to actually putting him down in singular form. His mythology is there, his personality (toned way down from previous drafts) and the world he lives in (i.e.: today). Taz's world is cut from Chandler's L.A., but isn't L.A., because I don't live in L.A. and don't know what L.A. is like. So Taz's unnamed city is an amalgam of Pittsburgh and the neighborhoods I grew up in. There are a lot of decaying old neighborhoods and hidden nooks and streets that haven't changed since the '40s. The villain of the piece is not necessarily the monster; the victim isn't necessarily the dead girl.

I think I surprised myself when I finished this story because before this, I thought very clearly in terms of "black and white" and "right and wrong". *The Naked Bones of an Echo*, originally called "Strangeways Detective", incidentally, led me down a mental and philosophical path I'd never traveled before, one of moral grey areas. Virtually every other story in this collection, particularly *Scrimshaw* and *Trapdoor*, grew from the new landscape introduced to me by completing this story. And it allowed me, then, to confront my own, very writerly fear: the fear of stagnation.

If every writer shares one attribute, it's the terror of mediocrity. Publishing is a rough business and a lot of writers don't make it through. It isn't the fear of rejection slips that makes most writers quit before they start, but the fear that the rejection slips might not only be personal, but true. That these slips might be saying, 'Sorry, pal, you're not as good as the hundred other guys knocking at my door and, you know what? You never will be.'

If there's a bogeyman lingering in every writer's closet, it's that one. And sometimes I think, maybe the reason I don't write much short fiction much any more has nothing to do with my current workload—that screenplay is more important and that article's deadline is more pressing. Sometimes, I'm afraid that I gave into the bogeyman of inadequacy. And someday, that's a fear I'm going to have to face.

And To All A Good Night

He came down the chimney just after midnight, as the clock turned Christmas Eve into Christmas Morning. Smiling, as the children, who had been hiding behind the furniture, rushed up to him with cries of joy, jumping for him with outstretched hands.

Beginning, as he always did, he gouged out their little eyes, yanked out their hair by the roots. He reached in and tore their tongues apart. Gleefully smiling with rows of razor teeth, he chewed open their throats, sliced off their ears.

Seizing hold of their legs, he ripped them in two, gnawing on the tendermeat drumsticks. He cracked open their bones and greedily sucked out the marrow, laying the clear white ends neatly in rows. Hand over hand, he pulled out the intestines, and did a joyous ribbon dance around the red-splashed room.

Then he rolled around in the gore, splashing playfully in the pools of wet like a happy baby in a tub. Then, laying a crimson dripping talon aside a flared slit nostril, he gave a wink of yellow eye, and a nod of mottled gray head, and up the chimney he rose, scaled and pitted tail trailing after him. Dash away, dash away to the next house filled with naughty children.

And good ones too…

R.E.M.

Unable to sleep, Joseph went traveling, and wound up invading a woman's dreams. That he did not know her made the violation all the more appealing to him. She was dreaming of herself, traveling on a train, alone, staring out the window, chin in her palm, watching the blurring and shifting scenery beyond the tracks. In life, she must have been much more plain than her dreamself, for the sculpted, raven-haired image itself kept shifting and blurring slightly, much like the passing scenery. Not enough to deter him, however.

She wore black lace gloves which barely reached her thin wrists, her legs clad in black nylons, black pumps adorned her feet. She was waiting for someone, he could see it. Joseph became that someone.

Neither spoke as he approached, smiling and sitting down in the seat across from her. Her mouth, painted crimson, formed an "o" of surprise. Leaning forward, he touched her face; the rouged flesh seemed very real beneath his palm.

There came a voice, very close, yet very distant, echoing louder the further away it got. It said "Tickets, please" or something else entirely. Without looking away from her face, Joseph reached into his inside pocket and gave the theater-usher a thin black book. Since the man was of her conjuring, and not his, he had no reason to face him. The theater usher went away. His footsteps receding, then disappearing entirely.

Joseph reached out to touch her with his other hand, bracketing her, holding her face between his palms, stroking her hair. They were the only people in the balcony, velvet ropes cut off their escape to their aisle to her right. No arm-rest separated them; their hips touched as her skirt, slit to her waist, rode up revealing flawless white thighs. His eyes held her gaze as easily as his hands embraced her head—his hands had grown much bigger, or else her head and body must have grown smaller, for he could hold her entire head in his palm. She was doing all the work; there was no need for him to shape her thoughts. Rather, he sat and waited for her sands to shift beneath their feet, swirling up around as the orchestra beneath them played on silently. Their movements were violent, the entire brass section lurched drunkenly as the strings section emptied itself of players one by one. The conductor held Joseph's book in his hand and he was waving it above his tiny, distant head. Joseph never had to look in the direction of the pit to see the scene; it was all there, played out in her eyes.

Proportionate to him once again, her hair was much redder now—no longer raven—almost matching her lipstick. He almost got the impression she was watching the scene unfold, floating above her body as her dreamself acted out the play. But there would be glimmers and flashes behind her now-blue, now-amber eyes, and he knew she was back inside her dreamself's head, looking out and watching him, returning his gaze. He could not see himself in her eyes. Occasionally, he saw her own face looking out at him, but he knew he was still himself.

Running his hand up her naked thigh, he reached beneath her green skirt and unhooked her garter belt, slowly pushing the nylon aside. She gasped, a rush of air, a tiny sigh, the orchestra played on. Hair dancing on the breeze, moving of its own accord.

Velvet ropes were actually attached to the arms of the couch, bolted to brass plates set in the sides, cruel blued steel hooks on the other end held them fast to the dark balcony, as it rocked and swayed on the ocean water. Blue-white water lapped at the top edge of the balcony, beneath the rail. The conductor had fallen against his podium far beneath them, sobbing. She took up his keening, hitching breath, as tears streamed down her cheeks. Mascara ran on one side, forming a tattoo of a black starburst around her emerald eye. His right hand was on her breast, beneath the black lace bra; her jacket had vanished. Her shoes were gone, her right foot buried in the sand. Slowly, gently, he eased her back onto the couch, red velvet covering sank beneath her shoulders, her left hand went into the black, unseen water. He heard the tiny splash and felt salt-spray in his hair.

On top of her now, caressing her naked breasts, biting her throat, she moans and claws his naked back. His tuxedo floats away, drifting languidly, then crazily on the breeze, but he does not watch. Instead, he thrusts his hand between her legs and she gasps, her eyes growing wide clenched tight. Images overlap as the room shimmers like curtains of night. There is applause all around them, but it fails to drown out the sobbing. Her tattoo has melted and run off her face, puddling beneath her head, streaking her hair as the rain beats hot on his back, spattering her face, droplets disappearing as quickly as appearing. The rain is coming from beneath them, falling up, or else they are hanging, suspended in midair, inverted and bound tight to the underside of the couch. Joseph couldn't get his bearings, but didn't allow the vertigo to overwhelm him. She was still beneath him.

Nipping at her neck, she dug her manicured, ragged nails into his shoulders, drawing blood, but not his. He thrust into her, though he was still clothed. She was naked save for the nylons, the gloves, the veil. He couldn't see her eyes beneath the sheer lace covering her face. She spasmed beneath him, he felt her legs lock around him, crossing her ankles at the small of his back, then around his neck. Impossibilities didn't bother him in the slightest. The sobbing was louder, echoing forth from her right ear. The right side of her face was very wet, the flesh puddled beneath his probing fingers.

There came a crack that sounded like a thunderclap, then a sigh which only served to increase the sobbing. She was beating her face with both hands, then her thighs. Her scream of anguish chased him, clawing at his back as he flung himself upwards, tearing himself out of her, hurtling headlong through the blackness. He left her wailing, seconds before she woke up.

In a tree, mere feet from the ground. A little balding, paunchy boy stood beneath him, looking up. Joseph could see his feet, dangling above the boy's hair. There were long shadows on the ground; Joseph searched the sky, searching behind fluffy clouds, but the sun was nowhere to be found.

"Comin' up?" Joseph asked. The boy nodded, jumping up, missing a branch. Joseph held one out to him, hoisting him onto the first limb, where he had sat.

"I can do it!" the boy protested, having grown smaller from the effort.

" 'kay," Joseph said, and sat back into the wood. He slid easily up and into the bark, slithering through it like mercury. The boy chased after him, climbing, his tiny, work-worn hands seizing branches, summoning the strength to haul himself onto each limb just slightly above him, his foot catching the one previously occupied by hand. Alternating fistfuls of wood and leaves, latticework of limbs, foliage obscuring all vision for a time, losing the boy in the tree. Joseph felt the boy's hands, tugging at him, at his wooden shirt, his leafy hair, seizing his wrists and his twigs in grasping handfuls.

Dangling in midair with no longer a foothold, the boy felt fear, then terror, then exhilaration at the fleeting thought of flying. Joseph felt the nourishment from the close proximity of the fear. Sometimes he hated this part of the traveling. Sometimes the regret was so bad his stomach rebelled and sleep avoided him for days on end—which was a vicious cycle, because he only went traveling when unable to dream on his own.

The boy sat on a branch next to him, picking leaves out of his hair and out of Joseph's. "Long way down," Joseph remarked.

"Not s'posed t' say that," the boy said, insulted. "Not s'posed t'even look down. But I always do!"

"Why?" Joseph asked, intrigued for the moment.

"Stupid," came the reply. Joseph wondered which one of them the boy meant.

The boy looked at him, with old eyes, fleshy pockets beneath. He was jowly, balding again. His fingers pudgy, swollen and cracked from the climb, sticky and stained green from the crushed leaves. A twig had pierced the flesh on the back of one hand. The hand sucked the twig in, greedily.

"Ew!" The boy shouted, and beat at his hand with the other, where the twig had gone in. It shot out like a spitball, then fell to the ground like a lead slug. With a sniff, the boy looked up; he still had a long way to go.

Standing, the pair stretched their arms above their heads, reaching out, on their toes, in synch. The boy wasn't preparing for the climb, just stretching. With a motion between a yawn and a sigh, and with a sad, sympathetic smile, which somehow read that it was for the boy's own good, Joseph took away the branch beneath their feet. The boy screamed and clawed for Joseph as he fell past him. Joseph didn't fall; he wasn't afraid of falling. More importantly, though an unnecessary addition: it wasn't his dream.

The boy hit a subsequent branch hard, felt his back split, his skin tear and bleed, pierced by the branch's thorns. It was wide enough to dance on, but it grew thin, rail thin, then it was gone and the boy was falling again. On the way down, he grabbed a passing branch, but then it was no longer in his grip and his fall was halted not in the least. Speed gained. In the movies, people fell slowly, as if time had no meaning, but the air was rushing past the boy, the balding, paunchy boy, the tiny, youth-kissed boy, branches beat at his face. There was nothing to hold on to, and the
ground was rushing up to meet him. Joseph wondered if the boy had a wife who loved him like his did.

(His wife was fast asleep beside him, stirring every now and then. Did the boy's wife sleep next to the boy? Or in another man's bed? Would she break his fall?)

The fall was long, never-ending. Yet it would halt soon, and Joseph knew better than to stick around in a falling dream for very long. There'd be no way out once the boy landed. Joseph leapt away.

He stepped into a room. A dark room. He could see himself, but there was no source of light to speak of. He knew only that he was not in his own head. The room seemed familiar.

With a thump, a harsh cone of white light enveloped him, and high above him was a hard white hole in the sky. He tried to shield his eyes from the light, but it burned right through his hand. He heard the crunch of steel on bone a nanosecond before the railroad spike punched through his skull. Just above his eyebrows, in the center of his forehead, the iron spike hit home, driving through the back of his skull, knocking him backwards off his feet. Bone shot in all directions. The pain was incredible, as blinding as the light. Blood, his blood, geysered out of the end of the spike, though it was not hollow.

His fall was broken by a cold metal table, which rang as the spike slammed through it, pinning him there. He could not sit up. The agony and the spike held him immobile against the table. And through the blood and pain and light he could see, high above him, standing out against the utter blackness, was an observation window. Dressed head-to-toe in surgical gowns and masks, were three women, though he knew it was the same woman in triplicate; he didn't have to see the face to know her. He almost smiled but the pain wouldn't allow it. Neither would she.

Her face suddenly loomed above him, a Rushmore addition, a gigantic, monstrous face with eternal brown eyes and cascading brown hair. The giant's head blocked out the observation window, the mouth opened, threatening to devour him whole. It was a gaping canyon, the gleaming teeth the size of boxcars, fillings, in the molars in the back, were manhole covers. Her pores were perfect.

Joseph clutched at the end of the spike with both hands, but it slid from his grasp, burying itself further in his skull. The grating squeal of metal on shattered bone raked across the inside of his head. He felt his teeth shatter to shards and powder in their sockets.

The head inhaled, the spike jerked, taking part of his brain with it, but it remained, holding him fast to the chrome table. "Knock it off and go to sleep!" She roared.

Eyes popping open, he rolled over, fighting nausea. The migraine and cold sweat finally subsided. It felt like hours, but the sickness held only for seconds. When his head cleared, he adjusted his covers, rolled over and kissed Lynn's neck. She smiled at his touch, but elbowed him anyway.

"Are you done traveling?" she demanded. It was an order.

"Alright, alright." He smiled and held her close. Absently, he began rubbing the center of his forehead; it throbbed slightly, and he could still remember the sickening sensation of iron grating against splintered bone. Yawning, he realized he was proud of her; she'd been surpassing even him lately.

It was a match made in dreams.

m.p.h.

I usually try to avoid the southern states altogether. Black man in a fast car, that's just asking for trouble from some good ol' boy trooper. But I can't always avoid it. Sometimes I need a change of scenery just so I don't go crazy. Midwest can be just as bad, though. Especially when I have to cruise at around 90 or 95 to keep them down and at peace. The speed keeps them quiet.

I've never had any trouble with the car. It wasn't cherry when I got it, and I've since spun the odometer back to zero, but it's never had so much as a flat tire or an overheated radiator, no matter how hard I drive it—and that's pretty hard, considering. Good mileage too, back and forth across the country, as long as it takes, all night, every night. Without stopping.

That's the stipulation: Can't stop at night. Not for more than a couple of minutes. Long enough to empty my bladder off the side of the road, if it's an absolute emergency. During the day, I gotta sleep, but it's alright to stop during the day. Pills help at night. Keep me awake, keep my appetite down, which is good. Because unless I can get work for a couple of hours sweeping up in some small town store for a couple of bucks, I can't always afford to eat much. When I do get money, usually spend it on crackers and juice. It keeps my strength up, helps me endure the damage from the pills and the time changes. And the long nights. Every night.

Some times, I can find a person who'll let me catch a few hours' sleep on their porch. Occasionally, even get a back room cot. On the rare occasions I have the money, I'll splurge on a one-day's stay at a boarding house, which is never too dear. Usually, though, it's me in the back seat, at the side of the road, hoping I don't bake in the sun.

All that driving, fast and frantic, all night, every night, I have too much time to think. Can't always find things to listen to on the radio, especially out in the middle of some desert highway, where the range isn't too good. Even so, the music doesn't drown out my brain, and I start thinking about Bennie, and the night I won the car from him.

Joey and I were fixing the roof on his mother's house when Bennie showed up out of nowhere, like magic. Hadn't recognized him at first; just another youngish black man in a cool ride, asking if we needed some help on such a hot day. We were a little suspicious at first, thinking he would try something, we didn't know what. But then I realized that I *did* know him, hadn't seen him in years, though, and he didn't have the Mustang then. He had been okay all those years ago, but we were just kids back then. He looked older than either of us now, and highway dust was imbedded in his skin. But we welcomed him up gladly, and he gave us a hand with the roof.

Joey brought out the cards at lunch and we played for the loose change in our pockets. I started a lucky streak I hadn't seen in ages, and was soon cleaning them out. Had almost two dollars in quarters at the end of the second game, and I started ribbing them, should I spend it all in one place, or stick it in a mattress for a rainy day. Just fooling around, having fun, after hard work and hot sun, downing lemonade and playing cards.

Then Bennie announced he wanted to play for cars. Sounded weird to me, and I didn't trust it. He driving around in that cherry-red Mustang and me in a beat up Chevy Nova that had more parts in the trunk than it did under the hood. Figured to me that the car was stolen.

But I wasn't about to call him on it. Actually, I didn't think he was serious. Neither did Joey. So we laughed and went along with the gag.

I don't wonder anymore if he threw that hand, 'cause I think of the laugh he let out when he lost. His laugh had none of that "I'll be damned" some men have when they lose. The laugh he let out seeing my two pair was one of pure and utter relief, as if he'd carried that car around on his back for years, and my threes and tens lifted it right off him. Laughed so hard he cried, and Joey and I figured something must have broken inside his head.

Now I had no intention of going through with this. I just saw it as a friendly game. Could have back his change, too, if he wanted it, I wasn't dirt poor. But he refused my "no thanks"; said a deal was a deal.

I understand completely now, of course, and I know what he told me. Can't let it sit at night. Can *not*. Faster you drive it, the better too. Speed keeps them down. And no, he wouldn't take it back. Not ever. Not for a million dollars.

"There's demons on the road," he told me, tears still glistening in his eyes. Tears of utter joy. "Some drive in the next lane, cut you off with inches to spare." He looked up at the sky and started to laugh again, his breath hitching in his throat. "Then there are the demons you take with you." Then he let out a whoop and jumped up in the air, like he was so happy to see the sky standing still at dusk. "Getting dark," he said to me, with almost an apology on his lips. "Better get going."

I didn't believe him then. Who the hell would? I just drove it around the block and parked it in the lot behind my house, sitting and listening to that powerful engine roar. Like sitting in the belly of a beast, and I couldn't believe it was mine. Really all mine.

I cut the engine, and a little while later that girl walked by. Behind the car. I know I hadn't been sitting there for more than a couple of minutes. But I hadn't believed a word Bennie had said. Thought he was crazy. So I called his bluff. I sat there alone in that car after full dark, feeling sort of like a fool, but a fool with himself a new Mustang. And just as it got full dark, that girl walked behind the car.

And I've never stopped it at dark since. Full dark and the car's parked, engine's cut: things get real bad. Screaming happens. And blood.

I've made mistakes. Fell asleep too long, let dark come. Once needed a bathroom break and was gone too long. That was in Raleigh. With the college kids sitting on the trunk, having a smoke. I was crying like a child when I left there, with blood still glistening on the chrome.

Sometimes, I'm tempted to stop when I'm real low on money. Just stop and wait and take what's left after. But I couldn't really do that, could I? This car is my responsibility now, and I am no murderer. But mistakes happen.

Then I think, to hell with it. Park it in the desert and let it rot. Push the evil thing over a goddamned cliff. That would do it, wouldn't it? Destroy the car completely. That should do it.

Problem was, I didn't know for sure. What if it didn't stop it? What if destroying the car just let them loose? No way to keep the car moving if it was destroyed, and it was the speed that kept them down. I couldn't risk it. Just couldn't. It's more than just me to worry about. It's everybody. Being ninety-nine percent sure of something, doesn't make you a hundred percent. So I just couldn't risk it.

So I drive all night, with the radio and the pills to keep me awake. On the back roads and on desert highways, you can get up past one hundred. And yeah, the whole car is a burden, but it's still a Mustang and it hasn't lost the thrill of being a Mustang. So I try to make the best out of a hellish situation.

So I was doing over a hundred when the flashing blue lights appeared in my mirror, and the piercing wail cut through the air. No way to outrun that sound. I shouldn't have been going that fast, not then. Save the real speed for full dark, that's always been my rule. But I was punchy. Couldn't sleep real well that day, too hot in the desert. Too many pills at once. Most of all, the lack of sleep almost made me forget why it was I drove at night. And why I drove fast only at night.

He was a tall white trooper, belly just starting to free itself of his belt. Called me 'boy' and told me to step out of the car as the sun started to sink down at the end of the road, setting the highway on fire.

Punchy, like I said. I should have just jammed on the gas right then and there, but it wasn't full dark yet. I thought I'd be safe for the time being. Get a ticket and be on my way. Wasn't thinking clearly. Should have been thinking more clearly.

He ran my plate as he made me stand there for a real long time. The sun was sinking fast, turning the sky to blood. When he came back, he looked like he'd just caught Jack the Ripper.

"Okay, boy, you just stay stiff as a board. We're gonna have a look in your trunk."

Nothing scared me so much in my entire life than those words coming out of his mouth. I couldn't move. I just stared at him like I didn't - couldn't - understand what he was saying. I saw that young girl in the back of my mind, walking around the back of the car. Heard the scream as she vanished from sight, her scream echoing through the inside of the car.

Trooper was holding out his hand to me, still talking, right hand on the butt of his pistol. "Now you're gonna give me your keys real slow."

I didn't move. My keys hung loose from my hand like they were a part of me I couldn't use.

"You hear me talking to you, boy?"

Redneck racist cop out of some rotten T.V. movie about Klansmen, telling me to hand over my keys. The outrage wasn't enough to snap me out of my trance. He unholstered his gun and kept it on me while he stomped over and snatched the keys away. "Guess you're deaf as well as fucking stupid, huh, killer?"

I blinked, trying to get a handle on his words.

"Yeah, we know all about you. You're wanted all over the country," he walked backward towards the trunk as he talked, gun still trained on me. A nervous hero grin started to form at the corners of his mouth. I expected him to giggle as he fumbled with the keys, trying to find the right one. Old Mustang, had regular-sized keys. All looked the same on that ring. "Murder," he was saying. "Kidnapping. Been real busy, eh, boy? Too busy to ditch your car? Or too fucking dumb?"

It felt like a dream. I was actually screaming at myself to wake up because it must be close to dark. But I was awake, and the sky was turning dark blue as the stars came out of hiding.

I haven't been stopped by a trooper in a long time. Couldn't even remember what state I was in.

Trooper found the key, the silver glinted in the taillight glow. He started to turn the key, started to open the trunk. I must have screamed for him to stop. I think he slammed my head down on the trunk. Next thing I knew, I was down on the ground, and my head hurt like it was on fire and the trooper was screaming at me to stay down just stay the fuck down. A little bead of blood had collected at the rim of the gun barrel. I could see it so clearly, barely inches from my face.

And I watched in utter horror and amazement as the trooper turned the key and lifted the lid of the trunk, just as the last traces of the sun disappeared from the sky. The best example of perfect cosmic timing I have ever seen.

The trunk lid made a perfect arc and bounced against its springs. The trooper didn't even have time to scream before the light poured out of the trunk and the wind howled and swept around him. And the hundred sets of talons reached out for him, clawing into his shoulders and face, ripping his skin, tearing, rending, dragging him into the trunk, his legs scissoring in the air, my keys and his gun dropping from his hand, clumping to the dust.

The scream came soon enough. I could hear him through the ringing in my head, as the blood poured out over the lip of the trunk like a fresh spring waterfall, crimson cascading over chrome.

No matter how many times I see it - even though I'm careful and it doesn't happen often - I cannot get used to it. How do you get used to seeing human beings ripped apart by things you're too scared to look at? I hear the screams at night. I see the thick grey texture of the muscled, taloned hands. The teeth and eyes glinting in the darkness. Eyes protruding through outstretched palms on some. The growling, gnashing, snarling over the whipping, howling wind. The blood soaking into the ground as nature accepted the offering from the unnatural.

Reflex made me leap up and slam the door closed on them before any could crawl out. But the car had been still for too long now, and they were rocking it deep from inside. Deep, deep inside. Shaking it so much that the shocks squealed, and it actually began to bounce as they pounded against the inside of the trunk.

My hand shook in one direction, the car in the other, and it was a struggle to get the key into the ignition, one try, two tries - and there! In, and with a brutal twist, a new roar was added to the awful, horrible howls inside.

I drove it smoothly back onto the road, leaving the trooper's headlights behind me, staring off into the full dark night.

I never had any trouble with the car. And I don't know why driving it at night keeps the gate closed, but it does, and I won't argue the point. Speed keeps them down. It's just a trunk during the day, but I still won't keep things in it. I try not to go back there if I can help it.

Maybe tomorrow I can find a place with a bath. That trooper's wallet is bound to be in the trunk somewhere come sun up. Maybe I can force myself to root around inside and find it, amidst the shredded clothes, old and new. Maybe I could use his credit card and treat myself to a hot meal. I hate to do it, but fair is fair. He stopped *me* after all.

Maybe, if I'm lucky, a truck will take a turn too wide and smear me and this car all over the road. Running from my problems, I know. Right now, though, this car is my responsibility. All night, every night.

I'll be able to stop come sun up.

In The Market for Souls

I was right on time, but I didn't have to be: he'd have waited. Just as he'd been waiting, hunkered down in the alley, in the dark. He'd've waited 'til the sun came up and blasted him into ashes, he didn't know any better. But I came and spared him, saved his life, if you could honestly call it that.

As soon as I had one foot in the alley, he was on me. Rushed up, shaking, his eyes wide and shining in the dark.

"You got it, man? Right?" he asked, desperation spilling from his mouth. "You got it?"

" 'Course I got it. Wouldn't be here if I didn't."

I opened my hand and showed him the two capped syringes. He made for them, but my fingers were faster and they closed around the tubes, hiding them from view. "What you got for me?"

His tongue lolled out. Wondered if I could be played. I could see it on his face. He was hungry enough, no doubt about it, but he hadn't been a 'breed that long, which is exactly why he needed me. The tongue licked at the new and sharp white canines. Then he pulled his lips over his teeth in a grimace, and his hand jammed into his pocket, coming out with a wad of crumpled bills, thrusted the wad at me.

It was enough, barely. I took the ball of cash and gave him what he needed. He wasted no time, ripping the cap off one and plunging the needle into his neck, a look of relieved ecstasy washing over his white dead face. Yanking the needle with one hand, the thumb fumbled to uncap the other. The cap shot off, he hurled the empty tube into the darkness, and made to plunge number two.

"No business of mine," I said as I was leaving. "But I'd save some. Price goes up next week."

He shot me a pained look like I'd just run over his dog, full of anger and misery. "No way! You can't do that!"

"Got to." I spread my hands wide in a typical gesture of 'What can I do?' "Folks been noticing here and there. Heat may be on. Ain't a public service, 'breed."

Panting, tongue licking out like a snake, he was going into a panic. "How much?"

I shook my head. "Don't know yet. I'll get the word out soon as I do."

"You prick," he said, getting shakily to his feet. He had some blood in him now, felt stronger, healthier, like he was human again. "I should just tear you up, get it over with."

I nodded. "Yeah, that would solve your problems." I turned and stared him down. One syringe gave him the strength to do me, yeah, but he didn't have it in him yet. Which is why we had the perfect business relationship. "You weren't so kill-shy in the first place, wouldn't be in this mess. Learn some fuckin' survival instincts, junior, or get used to the dark and get used to me."

He didn't like that. Didn't think he would. He growled and faded back a bit, into the dark where I couldn't see him well, then he lunged, his hands coming into the dim streetlight first. But I had my own hand up before he closed the gap. Crosses and holy water and all that movie shit only works on these idiots if you believe in it. Human faith. They lost theirs at rebirth. I don't believe in any of that shit, personally, so I held up my own talisman, giving him a quick burn on the forehead, making him yelp and jump back. Holding his hand up to the smoking patch of flesh, his growl was gone, but he was still glaring at me. I smiled, didn't even singe the ten-spot I burned him with. Everyone has their own gods.

I jammed my ten back into my pocket, shot him a look of disgust and pity for good measure and turned my back on him, just to show him what I really thought of him. "See you next week, 'breed. Do me a favor and pass the word around."

He didn't like that either, but what could he really do about it?

Vampires are a lot cooler in the movies. They're smoother, better looking, dress better, scarier. Even the punks in these new movies have more style that the 'breeds I deal with every night. These rotting, stinking morons who still think they're human, still think they feel human. Afraid to kill or even feed on live blood. Can't go out in the sun, think they should be afraid of garlic, for Christ sakes? What is that? It's like a human afraid of his own shadow 'cause some one told him it could hurt him. These 'breeds don't even know how to be what they are. Too scared to go sunbathing and get it over with.

Who knows how they got like that. Million different stories. Sloppiness by the 'bloods that made them, most like. Doesn't matter. As long as they can pay for the blood, I don't care if they evolve or die come morning. Once the money's in my hand, it ain't my worry.

I was telling the truth before, about the price jack-up. Buddy of mine's a paramedic, gets me what I need by siphoning some off his riders. Rest I can get through work, if I really need it. I get it from work, I can't charge as much. I'm a day morgue worker. My job to empty the corpses of their own fluid, and pump them up with the embalming kind. 'Breeds like blood from lifers; dead blood's too stale for 'em, but generally, they'll take what they can get. Risks are different in this case. I don't worry about getting caught 'cause it's all refuse anyway. It's a haz-mat thing, but I'm reasonably sure anyone saw me'd look the other way. Even if they didn't, it's no big deal, really. Just you can't always know what's *in* the blood this way. 'Breeds who haven't killed yet are still susceptible to human diseases. Overly so, in some cases. No immunity yet. But then again, there ain't many who care, either. They know the risks. Hunt or get it from me. Only choices.

Dane and Cobalt caught up to me in the bar. I needed a few before I went home, and midway through my second, they came right up behind me. They looked as pissed off and self-righteous as usual. I think they figured out I'd been avoiding them and their little lectures.

Dane was a huge black guy - or 'blood, or whatever you want to call him when he ain't around. Mean-looking, but slow to bare the fangs. Cobalt used to be a hot club chick, and still was, in a lot of ways. Eternally sixteen, hair dyed 'black number one', leather and chains and silver over cleavage. I liked looking at her, even when she was giving me shit, which was every time I saw her.

"Stivic—" Dane started, a deep growl of social conscience.

"I know, Dane," I said, not looking up from my beer. I could see them in the mirror. They weren't pulling their tricks tonight, not in a crowded lifer bar.

"You know, but you persist," he went on. I coulda mouthed it with him. First time I crossed with Dane, I thought he was trying to shake me down for a cut, like a pimp for 'breeds. But was worse: a neighborhood watch, helping the 'breeds off the streets with tough love and all that feel-good lifer shit. Dane and Cobalt were new gen' 'bloods, wanted to teach the 'breeds to hunt for themselves. Teach them the gentle art of what they called 'tapping' - getting lifer blood without making more 'breeds. Population control. Safe feeding. Social responsibility. And I'm the scum of the Earth.

"They don't buy from me, they buy from Willy, or Little Bob." There weren't many of us, obviously, but it was more than just me raping and pillaging out there.

"Willy's dead." That came from Cobalt. First time she spoke since they came in. I stopped, mid-swig, and turned around to look at her. She was easy on the eyes, but I wasn't sight-seeing just then.

"What happened to Willy?"

"Barlow and 'Sil," she said. "And Savin. And that whole group. They decided they didn't want him around any more."

"Unanimous vote," Dane said. "They're cleaning up the nights."

I felt a little cold. Willy was a goofball, but he was alright. *Had been*, anyway. Barlow and that bunch were mean. Old school 'bloods. Top of the line hunters. Used to do it for fun before they got civilized.

"Doing this serious, Stivic. Cobalt and I can't protect you anymore."

"I wasn't aware you two were my guardian angels."

"Only thing keeping you above ground is you haven't passed any bad blood lately."

"Hey, my stuff's clean. Quality, man. I even siphon off myself from time to time, rather than give tainted shit."

"Yeah, you're a prince," Cobalt said.

"You want to keep pushing, that's your business," Dane said. "You got no one to answer to now, Stivic. You are now without a net."

And then they were gone. 'Bloods are fast when they want to be. Faster than human sight. They wanted to remind me of that.

Shit. Dane and Cobalt were pains in the ass, but Barlow and that bunch weren't ones to piss off. I knew them by reputation only, never met a one of them. But a few years back, one of their private clubs got raided by some hopped up lifer group who found them somehow. Tore the place up with long bows. They got tore up even worse, though, when they stopped to re-load. And since then, the unspoken truce 'Bloods have with lifers has been a bit thin. If Barlow and Savin are cleaning up, then lifers like me gotta tow the line 'til the heat dies down. 'Bloods don't kill their own, but they'll rip me any day they think I'm trouble.

I don't think I'm trouble, just trying to make a buck is all. Not that they'd see it that way. I finished my beer and got the hell out of there, just in case I was in high demand that night.

Message on my answering machine wasn't good. I had a big night coming up. Lotta regulars in need of a fix. Fridays are always good for a grand at least, but I was running low on stock. I pressed the flashing button and heard the voice of my buddy, Ron: my supplier and partner.

"Dude, this is Ronny. Listen, I mighta gotten busted tonight. Gotta new partner with high ideals. Might be nothing, just a blow up, but I better lay low, just to make sure. Hope you got enough to hold you a week or two. Later."

Of course. My luck had been going too good for too long. Something had to change. Can't ride a wave forever. But I was low, real low. Almost out of the good stuff. Which meant either I was tomorrow's cow, or I hope for a really good couple of stiffs. And the way things were going, I could see hoping was for suckers.

I don't like needles, I'm a real pussy when it comes to them. The line I gave Dane wasn't bullshit; I've tapped myself a couple of times in the past, when I was just starting out. It hurt, and it took a million tries to find the vein. I don't know how the fuck junkies do it. I almost pass out every time. Most times, I can't do it at all. So I wasn't too fond of the idea of tapping myself to get my big score. I'd have to play tomorrow by ear.

They fished two homeless guys out of the river the previous night. That's all I got. I didn't like the downward course my life was taking.

'Breeds don't scare me; they're weak and sick, they haven't the foggiest freaking idea what they're actually capable of. But without a fix, even the biggest pacifist on the street is bound to get irritable. I told myself they were depending on me, that I was keeping them alive 'til they learned. But what'd I say before? I ain't the Red Cross. I wanted the money. I've held out before on 'breeds who couldn't pay.

I wanted the money and I'm chickenshit of needles. So I siphoned off the two old bums.

The blood came out thin, watery, more riverwater and Mad Dog than hemoglobin. It had an odd odor to it I didn't like either. Had a weird color, even for dead blood.

It was shit. I knew it. Took it anyway.

My first 'breed that night took the syringes greedily and I took off before he used them. I'd mixed the dead blood in with the remaining good stuff, shuffled the syringes around so I wouldn't know. Maybe I could make it last a little, or at least, make it look like it wasn't done on purpose. Thin, yeah, I know. But I tried to tap myself. I mean, I *really* tried. Couldn't do it, man. Got sick at the sight. Couldn't get the syringe anywhere near the vein.

So I made haste after every sale, couldn't watch them stick themselves. Didn't know what the bad stuff would do and didn't want to find out. I had twenty-three customers buying two tubes each. I'm supposed to drain myself of all that? Come on.

Halfway through the night, my path doubled back and I stumbled over one of the evening's previous buyers.

He was sitting on the ground, propped up against the side of the building, and had both needles sticking out of his neck. I prayed to God that 'breeds can o.d. Take it too fast or too much, whatever. But I knew they couldn't. His eyes were wide open, yellow, staring, still shining in the sliver of streetlight knifing through the dark. Thick black and bloody vomit caked around his mouth and chin, down the front of this shirt. His mouth was open, I could see the four sharp canines poking up beyond the other teeth.

My mind ran through its litany of denials. 'I didn't force him to take the stuff, he used too much at once'. My favorite, my battlecry: 'He would have just bought from someone else'. Whatever. Even if it wasn't the blood, it didn't look good for me. I sucked it up, though, tried putting it out of my mind as I headed for my last sale.

My last 'breed was a customer named Quick. Ex-lifer gang-banger you wouldn't think would have night-sweats about killing for food. I guess capping someone in a drive-by is easier than drinking a guy's blood.

Quick looked even jumpier than usual when I met him at our usual place. It could have been the flickery fluorescent lighting in the all-night McDonald's restroom, but he looked like complete shit.

"So, what, you're like the grim reaper now?" he demanded, keeping his back to the wall as I closed the door behind me. I played it cool, even as my stomach jumped and I felt my dinner backing up.

"What are you on? You got my money?"

"Fuck no! And stay away from me with that shit. You know you already killed six brothers? You on a killing spree or something?"

"Six!? What are you talking about?" Jesus H. Christ—*six*!

"Passing bad blood, motherfucker! It ain't like we can kick the habit, you son of a bitch! We need that to fucking live!"

I had to keep a grip, keep making like I had no idea what he was talking about. Leveled my gaze, got out the needles, said, "So, you don't want yours tonight?"

"Not that shit!"

I stuck the syringes back in my pocket. "Fine. See you 'round."

"Hey! Hey, man!"

I stopped, half-turned, cool as hell. "Change your mind?" I was pissing myself. *Six* dead. I was toast. Have to get out of here. Leave for a while.

"I got wise to you, motherfucker. You heard of a bad-ass bitch named 'Sil?"

Dead. I was fucking dead.

"She coming for your ass, shitdick. She gonna get me off your ticket. Take me in. Take you out."

"Good," I said, hoping my voice wasn't shaking as badly as my hands were, jammed into my pockets 'til they were ripping through the lining. "Maybe she'll give you some brains. Or at least some balls. Make you a 'blood and stop being a pussy." Big words from a corpse.

He just smiled, showing me his teeth. "You goin' down, Stivic. Poisoning 'breeds, must have a death wish."

"It wasn't poison! They couldn't handle it!" I was losing it. He wasn't even listening, climbing up and out the window, shimmying up the slick, stained, broken-tile wall like a tarantula.

"Chew you up, Stivic," he said, almost giggling. "Spit you out."

"They'da bought from someone else," I said for like the fiftieth time that week. "I'm not the only one selling!" I backed against the wall, behind the door, as far as I could from his retreating back, from the open window, now empty of Quick.

"Have a nice night, chump." And he was gone.

I ran over to where he'd been. Jumping as I yelled, to get to the high-set window. "Tell them I never passed bad blood before! This was a bad batch! Quick! It was a mistake, you know me, man! I'll make it all up! Two weeks for free! Quick! Quick!"

Nothing. He'd vanished, and I'd completely lost it. I pressed my cheek against the cold hard tile, squeezed my eyes tight to make it all go away. I was so dead. So stupid. Pissed, scared, frustrated, greedy, stupid. A rage settled over me and before I knew what I was doing, I picked up the plastic trashcan and began smashing it against the mirror over the sink, spilling garbage everywhere and yelling "Shit! Fuck!" and variations of the two.

Then some old rent-a-cop heard the noise and came in, hand on the butt of his gun, but I threw down the trashcan and bolted past him. Once I got outside, I rounded the corner, got into the dark as fast as I could, forgetting that that was the worst place to hide from 'bloods. I don't even know if I cared just then. Panting, swearing, I ripped the last two syringes out of my pocket and hurled them down the alley as hard as I could, then taking off before I heard them land, shatter in the darkness.

It suddenly dawned on me - I don't know why - but I had one last chance. Something Dane told me a long time ago, or maybe something I already knew from dealing with 'breeds and 'bloods these past two years. 'Bloods don't touch 'bloods. Or 'breeds. They don't kill their own, not like lifers. My one way out was to ditch being a lifer. To join up. Get a sponsor, a 'breed I was still down with, offer myself up. Get out of this mess, I was that fucking desperate.

Couldn't be a 'breed, though. Too new at it. Might take too big a bite, or suck too long, then I'd be done anyway. A 'blood, though. A 'blood would do it right. Make me. That'd be my shield. Save my ass. Then I could buy into Dane's crusade, or offer Barlow my services, even. Hell, I knew all the 'breeds, even the ones who hide down deep, hide from everyone. The 'bloods *needed* me to help their reform thing. Everyone knows: Stivic knows every 'breed.

So I took off, ran as hard as I could, checking every lifer club I'd ever seen Dane in. Every little nook I'd ever run into Cobalt. Went to the places 'bloods liked. All the while, feeling the shadows closing in. Every alley had eyes looking out, watching me. Barlow's little coven, his inquisition.

My paranoia had me in a vice grip. I looked around me, behind me, stumbling over my own feet as I ran, not bothering to chit-chat with any lifers who spotted me, oblivious to the fact that there were monsters all around them, every night. Not privy to the information I had. I knew though. Savin could be right above me, floating invisible over my head, keeping right up with my hysterical run. 'Sil, clinging ass-to-the-wall, past my line of sight, watching, waiting to reach out and tear open my throat, spill my blood into the gutter.

Barlow's group were serious 'bloods, doing the comic book parlor tricks. Some of them were centuries old, still knew how to become smoke or a wolf whenever they wanted. Could slide through the cracks of doors the width of a knife blade. They didn't fall for the garlic tricks. The faith thing didn't faze them much. Who cares about what lifers believe when you were around before they were out of the trees? They were fast. Eye-blink fast. Hit a light switch and cross the room before it got dark. They could be on the ceiling, or in the wind. They were the monsters in the closet. They were all your fears in one box. Shadows with sharp teeth.

I needed Dane. I needed Cobalt. They weren't friends, but they wouldn't offer me up. I needed them to protect me from the monsters.

Finally, I found them. Rather, they found me. Before I knew what was happening,—running down Furnace Ave., heading for the Cellar Club – the wind whistled, cold all around me, and then I was dumped on my ass on a rooftop, looking out over the city and the river, the lights gleaming and twinkling far below me and into the distance. I could only see the two of them: Dane and Cobalt. But I knew they weren't alone. There were others in the darkness of the rooftop, watching us from the shadows, wanting no part of me.

Nobody spoke. Down on the street, life went on. Cars honked, people shouted. Music drifted up from the clubs. But it was still on the roof. I couldn't talk; too freaked out by the seemingly instant trip. They just stared down at me like I was some kind of new bug. Dane's eyes were blank, expressionless, but Cobalt's burned with fury. They both seemed very beautiful and alien to me just then. I realized I was actually looking at them for the first time. The facts became very clear to me, and I gasped out loud as the realization struck home, as if I had just now come out of some drug fog. They were a completely different race of creature, man-shaped. I'd seen the 'true-faces' of 'bloods before, but the reality never hit me like this. They were *not* human. They were the most inhuman species you could think of. When I came across a 'breed for the very first time, I didn't think about were they human or not; my only thought was 'how do I cash in on this'? How do I make a buck?

I was still panting, but I turned away from them, from their beautiful frightening faces, and looked down over the edge of the building, seeing the streets so far away, and the city all at once. And then my situation became that much more real. I was having a true moment of clarity here. And I didn't like what I was seeing. "Listen," I gasped, pleading, still on my knees, all ready to beg. "You gotta help me, Dane," I turned and looked up at them. What's the word? Beseechingly. "Cobalt, you know me. I don't pass bad blood. Please, they're coming for me."

"Can't help you, Stivic," Dane said simply, and without emotion.

"It was an accident, Dane. I swear to Christ! You gotta believe me. I mean, it was like bad karma, you know? You say I don't pass bad blood, then what happens? I get a bad batch without knowing it, I mean, I didn't *know*, you know? I mean, how could I know?" I was talking fast. Not a grifter rap, but the panicked stream of words. Desperation pouring out.

"It was filth," Cobalt's voice, hard, cold. "You should have staked them out in the sun. It would have been kinder."

"It was bad luck," I insisted, not hearing her. "I didn't know. I didn't mean to hurt them!"

"Don't!" Cobalt spat, bringing her face dangerously close to mine. She seized my lapels and yanked me up on my knees. "Don't even think it! You didn't care about any of them! They were weak, and you wanted their money! You preyed on them! You could have helped them."

I was getting mad, now. I was running out of time and resented having to defend myself. "Hey, Cobalt. Don't lay that trip on me. You should have gotten to them the minute they turned 'breed. I was the only thing keeping them alive."

She started to answer back with a snarl and a closed fist, but Dane stepped in.

"We told you, Stivic, we're through with you. You coulda gone seven different ways with those 'breeds, including staying out of their lives altogether. But you played your sick dealer games and now you gotta pay for them."

He turned away, started to walk towards the shadows. Cobalt dropped me and went to follow. I was on my hands and knees, scrabbling after them. "Look, wait—" I grabbed Dane's hand, begging. "I'll make it right. I swear. Put the bite on me, I'll make up for everything. Everything. Just give me another chance, please. I know them. All the new ones. You'll never find them all. There's too many. They're sick, Dane. Dying. Please, I'm begging you, Dane, please. Make me! Don't let Barlow kill me, please."

He shook me off and kept walking, but I couldn't stop myself. "You don't even have to make me. Just take me in. Just 'til the heat's off. I'll take you to every 'breed, man. Every one. I'll never deal again.

And I'll give back. They can tap me if they need to. Look, look, you can see it, can't you? I'll do anything you want, Dane, just don't leave me to them!"

They stopped and looked down at me like I was nothing. A worm. Then, all of a sudden, we were the *only* ones on that roof. The others, the ones who couldn't be bothered to show themselves to a worthless lifer, they were all gone. I couldn't feel them in the shadows, on the back of my neck. Just the three of us now. I looked up, willing to promise my soul to Dane. "Please," I whispered, too hoarse now to raise my voice.

Then they were gone too. I was too scared to cry, too tired to run. My knees gave out and I slumped over, dragged myself the few feet back to the wall, crammed myself into a dark corner of the ledge. Behind me and below me, Barlow and his friends were looking for me. And they'd find me, no matter where I hid, and whether Dane told them where I was or they looked for me themselves. I wasn't even good as food to them. This was a vengeance game. I was marked, a dog to be hunted down. I sat and stared into the shadows and waited.

I didn't have to wait long. I couldn't see them, any more than I could see Dane's companions when they were there. But I knew they were there, and I'd see them soon enough, though I did not want to. They were definitely there, in the shadows, watching me. They'd come for me slow, and hurt me slow.

They were going to have me for dinner and never touch a drop.

Waiting for the Man

It was just the four of us sitting in the bar, guns on the table, when the man in the black suit walked in. Without thinking, I pumped four shots into his chest. He hit the floor like a wet rag and lay still, bleeding all over the scarred wood. I knew he'd come for me eventually; I just hadn't expected it to be tonight.

As I set my gun down like a dope and looked away from the brand new corpse, I found myself staring down the end of Darryl's gun. My heart jumped, but I don't think my face betrayed me. "Where were we?" I asked, calmly, coolly. I'd just killed a man, but you couldn't tell by looking at the others. Darryl just glared at me, as twitchy as usual. Angel looked annoyed at having been interrupted. Murray just sat in the corner, trying to blend in with the shadows.

"We're taking the money, Ben," Darryl said, his gun trembling slightly in his outstretched hand. His other hand crept slowly towards the bulging pillowcase on the floor in front of him, its mouth tied shut with a length of clothesline.

"I thought that was already decided," I said, not liking the way his hand was shaking. "For all intents and purposes, you two are dead," I nodded towards him and Angel. Her lips were set in a pissed-off pout. She didn't like having decisions made for her. She'd expressed her dislike before. The knot above Darryl's left eye was beginning to heal up a little, but it still looked painful as hell. I continued, hoping to talk him into putting his piece away. "No one in the world knows you two are alive. We made sure of that. You can go anywhere you want.

Tino'll find the pair of cinders in the car any day now. No one'll know different." I smiled what I hoped would be a disarming smile.

"You will," he said. Darryl's hand was shaking harder. The kid was losing it. We all knew it, including him. I could smell the dead man's cologne coming in on a breeze through the open window behind me.

Murray still hadn't said a goddamned word. It was my fault he was in this. No it wasn't. I told him I didn't need or want his help. He pushed anyway. Maybe Wanda was right and he is in love with me. His devotion was touching at times, considering we hadn't known each other all that long. Also considering the hopelessness of his love for me. Once, a woman loved me that unconditionally. I hadn't deserved it then, either.

Angel uncrossed her long legs and stood up, stretching. Darryl shot her a look. "Sit down!" he ordered.

She glared at him and continued standing. The kid's eyes darted from me to her and back. Twitchier. He decided to ignore her—a feat at which we all knew he'd fail, but he gave it a go anyway. He knew what it meant to take his eyes off her. It happened twice, then I got stuck with her. But I hadn't realized how stuck at the time.

"No way we can let you live, Ben. Or Murray. You'd be on the horn to Tino in a second." Darryl was talking fast. Angel stretched her arms above her head and arched her back, like she hadn't a care in the world. Her long black hair tumbled down over her back. My full attention was on her out of the corner of my eye. Not even a gun could keep me from watching. And I hated myself for it, because she was going to kill me one way or the other. Maybe she loved me too. Probably not. My initial reaction to her was probably correct: she only cared about herself, and then not even that much. She had enough hatred to spill out across the world and still have plenty left over for herself.

Darryl's eyes kept flicking back to her. He knew she was toying with him—or maybe he didn't. He hadn't figured it out as of yesterday, though we could see it. It was working in my advantage, however. Every split second his eyes were on her was a split second I could lean forward, bare inch at a time, closer to my own gun. The gun I was dumb enough to set down because I didn't think the kid had the grit to pull his. Why didn't I see it now? I'd figured him out before. All the signs were there. Lack of brains equals overcompensation in the guts department. But I'd been too tired and too dumb and too sick of life for too long. Just when I started caring about furthering my own existence, the whole world crashed down on my head again. It was almost funny.

Neither Murray nor Angel had yet said a word since we'd sat down. I thought about the whole stupid thing. From Anna's death all the way up to now. That bullet had been meant for me, instead it got her. Mrs. Ben, dead for no reason. That part of my life had been before her time, before we met. Before she agreed to marry me. Before she loved me. And because I was a tough guy as a kid, my sins were visited on her head. Made me give up on my own life.

So then what do I do? Hire out an old friend to find a guy to hunt me down. Anna hadn't seen death coming, why should I, right? Melodrama, I was in love with it. When guilt turns into self-hate, you stop feeling sorry for yourself, but you just can't help ringing down the curtain in front of an audience. It wasn't enough for me to want to end my own life; I had to get someone to do it for me. Who the hell takes out a contract on their own head? I guess, to my mind, it was something in between poetic justice and a private joke. Anna's insurance had left me plenty of money. Enough to get the job done, with the stipulation that they wait. So I can live in fear. So I can suitably punish myself.

Then Wanda takes me in. New city, new faces. New me, soon to be dead me. Wanda has a habit of taking in strays—that's where Murray came from. Nowhere, like me. So now I got friends again, who don't ask, but figure I'm in the middle of a long banshee wail. So they do their best to cheer me up and keep me from walking in front of buses in my own self-inflicted haze. Keeping me waiting for the man, without asking me why.

Then that stupid kid shows up. Stupid from day one. The worst kind of stupid: the kind that thinks it's smart. I can identify very well with that particular brand of idiocy. And he has Angel with him. She's in the passenger seat, but everyone could see she was driving. So he was her way out, away from Tino and his hard-time band. Her ticket out of slavery was someone too dumb to realize he was running the railroad. She let him think he was *the* man. You'd think he would have seen it before, in a movie, or on TV., it was such an old setup. The minute she could, she'd leave him far away.

But he had his story too. She'd twisted his head around, got him to think it was his idea to rip off her former "master". Tino might not have been much smarter than Darryl, but he was a hell of a lot meaner. He got to the top and stayed there this long. No idiot son with pocket change was going to take him down. Angel had hooked up with Tino sometime between Daddy's choir-girl and race-track whore. She became kept princess, with a pouty look and come-hither thighs, raking in green and spending it quick when the big boy's back was turned, putting up with the smack in the mouth or the belt on the rump as long as she felt the ground would be solid. The minute she stood on mud, however, she'd start looking for a new boy.

I didn't know all the details. Women like her only give the Reader's Digest "Tell a Lie" version. But Tino must have changed his attitude towards her, growing eyes in the back of his head. She couldn't take the surveillance. Made her felt trapped under too many hot blankets. So the dreamer comes along. Just lucky enough to still be alive. Never upright on a rug for too long before his feet hover over his head and he crashes down again. But he's wheels out, and cute enough to bear the tough-guy gab. So she puts him behind the wheel, gives him the keys and "thanks for the lift, mister". And they take off with ten grand.

But Captain Brains doesn't figure that the rest of the world is brighter than him. And without Angel pulling his strings, he limps into a bar, flies out with a new black eye and ten grand in the hole. The whole world can see a jerk coming, traveling under their own neon sign pointing down at the knobby head and happy-sap smile. Gets his pocket picked and clock cleaned. Then he and Angel are in plain sight. Soon it'll be just him, with her leading the bloodhounds, sobbing behind Tino with "that brute" stories that change for the worse every ten feet or so. All of a sudden, Darryl's the new favorite fertilizer unless he can figure a cash-scheme quick.

But alive isn't good enough. He needs the girl, too. She's the only thing that will let him stand apart from the other jerks of the world. She's the only thing that makes him a man. So into another empty town they go. Empty save for me.

And then I fall for the line. My gut reaction is to send them both on the highway again, with a map to some other sucker. Just drink your beer and wait for the man, I think. But I don't. Because Angel has green eyes, just like Anna had. The exact shade. A pair of emeralds lying beneath a suspended cage, with no one around for miles. I took the bait.

And then she had me tied as tight as the kid. Only I was old enough to know better. I should have chucked one of us out the window that first night. But I fell for the green eyes and the garter belt, and the black nylons with the seam in the back. Oh yeah, I fell for the "Darryl's down in the bar, crawling under a beer. And who cares if he knows anyway? I hate him." Not to mention the true trigger: "You'll protect me, won't you?"

I couldn't protect my wife. Maybe this was the Big Second Chance I'd been secretly hoping for, like the jerks on television. I was a television jerk, alright. The famous ones get better writers when they paint themselves into corners, though. I was out of commercials. And of course, I knew all this going in. And in. In bed, in cahoots, in up to my neck. Insane.

So instead of waiting for the man, I did the job. My memory was murky, but I remembered being good at the acquisition of other people's money when I was a wee lad. The two stiffs came as a lucky break courtesy of a local love-murder-suicide. (He was a heel, but he was *her* heel. None of us had anything to do with it. But we heard the shots, and my mind was already working. So into the trunk went Sonny and Cher, oozing all over the inside and all over us, but the next day was the job, thirty miles away. Who'd miss Sonny and Cher anyway? They had each other now.)

I couldn't get Murray to stay out of it though, so he became our wheelman. What was there to like about me? I couldn't figure him out. Now I've just as likely gotten him killed.

The job went without a hitch. I was sure that Darryl'd get jumpy and kill someone, a teller or a guard, but he kept as cool as it was possible and no one got hurt. And when we got back to Wanda's bar, that's when the guns came out, with the pillow-case full of money in the middle of it all.

"You're going to kill us?" I asked, as Angel continued exercising her long legs behind "her man".

Darryl nodded to my question, unable to look at Angel, but unable to keep a fixed gaze on me either. His distraction allowed me a couple inches gain on my own gun, stupidly placed a thousand miles away. "Why?" I asked. Darryl's eyes snapped back to me.

"Why *what*?"

"We don't want your money. I don't want it. Murray doesn't want it. The only one's who want it are you two. So why kill us for something you already got?"

"Like I said," Darryl licked his lips, sweat was pouring down his face. It wasn't that hot in there. "You know we're alive. No one can know."

"Who am I going to tell? They'll come after that guy when he doesn't show," I nodded towards the corpse in the black suit, "and I'll be right back where I started."

"Why did you kill him?"

All eyes jerked towards the bar. It was the first time Angel had spoken since we arrived. I'd forgotten she had a voice, smoky and thick. She brushed a stray hair from her face and looked at me. I just stared back.

"You've been waiting for him for how long?" She went on. "A year? More? You want to die, Ben. Why did you kill the man who'd be doing you a favor?"

Until she asked, I hadn't given the matter any thought. I wasn't about to tell her that for a split second, I forgot all about my guilt, my pain. I was thinking of her. In spite of myself, I didn't want to die until I was certain she'd be alright. Darryl wasn't the jerk, I was. I've been waiting a long time to die, and for a weird minute, I wasn't quite ready. And I still wasn't ready, not to die at the hands of some small-time nothing like Darryl. Not even at her hands, which I was sure it would come down to. But I'd be damned if I'd tell her that.

"Forgot myself for a moment," I lied. I don't think that was the answer she was looking for.

"Come on, Ben. Tell me. You ready for life again?" She said, arching a thin eyebrow, curling a thin smile out of her pouty red lips.

"Does it really matter?" I asked. She looked hurt for a second. I didn't dwell on it. Instead, I jerked my head towards Murray, who was still silent in the corner, wearing an unreadable expression on his face. I hadn't thought much about him the past year. The stray giant Wanda had found as the new bartender half a year ago. I liked him well enough —though not as well as Wanda thought he'd like me to. Soon he was watching out for me, too. He called himself my friend on many occasions. The whole reason he followed me into this stupid mess. If I was smart, I would have stayed with Murray from the beginning.

"Why don't you let Murray go?" I said. "He's not about to tell anyone about you. I don't think he really cares two blinks whether you live or die."

Darryl shook his head, almost violently. "Forget it." He whirled on Angel. "And will you sit down!" he shrieked at her. They glared at each other for a split second, but it was all I needed to dart forward and grab my gun unnoticed. I dropped my hands beneath the table and waited a second longer.

Long enough for Angel to break his gaze and pull her own gun. She fired five shots wildly, but Darryl took every one. His back was to her, but his head was turned around. Two of the shots went into his shoulder, near his neck, tearing out his jugular on the way through. The third slug shattered his jaw; the fourth went in just above his eye and ripped through beneath his nose, showering teeth across the table.

The fifth was a little off: it went into his wrist, severing his hand. The bloody mess that had been a twenty-five year-old knucklehead slid to the floor, his blood mixing with that of the heap across the room. A little crimson lake was forming in the center of the room.

Angel stepped forward and placed a slender, manicured hand on the pillowcase. I should have fired then, because as her eyes ticked towards me, she opened another volley of shots. Three came nowhere near me, but the fourth punched my shoulder and knocked me out of my chair. My own gun went flying. I heard it hit somewhere in front of me. It made a heavy splash.

I had barely landed on my back when I heard the answer to Angel's assault. The shots echoed from my right, from the shadows. Bright flashes of white light threw her shadow on the wall as her body contorted with the shots. Finally, she flew into view, landing face down in the thick lake in front of me, just to the left of the corpse in black. Her emerald eyes stared at me, blood trickling from her temple, sliding through the trench of her lips, then pattering onto the floor beneath her. The lights went out of her eyes and I realized she wasn't seeing me anymore.

The throbbing in my shoulder had my whole body in a vice grip, but I forced my sand-filled head to turn, to stare up at Murray, who was just then coming out of the shadows. The light from the bar slashed across his face. He looked down at me, sad smile and sad eyes. He was a giant holding a smoking toy gun.

I tried to choke out a response, a thank you, a question, a why, but there was too much blood in my mouth: I'd bitten a chunk out of my tongue on the way down. Murray knelt down, then sat down next to me. He examined my shoulder.

"Clean through," he said. And smiled. It was a weird smile, but one I was used to seeing from him, but only when he thought I wasn't looking. I'd caught the smile a number of times. The first time, I had to have Wanda explain it to me, because I didn't know everything.

"She was no Anna," he said. And sighed, glancing around at the sources of all the blood on the floor. Everything was scattered. Murray smiled again. "She wasn't worth more pain, Ben."

I tried to speak, but more than blood was closing my throat. I wanted to agree, to say I was an idiot. That a beautiful face and green eyes was enough to make me forget, for a moment, that I wanted to die. I couldn't, so I nodded. And I let Murray interpret for himself. "I'll call an ambulance, then the sheriff," he said, giving my knee a reassuring pat. "I'm sure he'll see this as a robbery. No worries." He smiled again at me, then hoisted himself to his feet. He took a step forward, then stopped. Almost as an afterthought, he reached into his jacked at pulled something out. He let this something slide out of his big hand and land next to me. It was an envelope. Old, yellowing, wrinkled from two years of staying inside someone's jacket pocket. It still contained a thick bundle inside. A bundle that I would bet had never been touched.

"Here's your money back, Ben," he said without looking at me. "I couldn't complete the job." There was another sigh. "Never found the right guy," Murray said, then walked with heavy steps towards the phone behind the bar, leaving me to stare at a pair of dead green eyes, and wonder who the dead man in black had been ten minutes before he stepped inside.

Valentine

It seems that my would-be suitor fancied himself as Van Gogh, judging from the ear I received in the mail. Wrapped in red tissue paper in a little heart-covered box. Melodramatic. And how very much like him: unoriginal.

I sent the ear back with a little note telling Ronald that self-mutilation was not the way to win my affections. If he insisted on giving himself to me, he could try to be a little more imaginative. A lady has to have standards, after all. Where would I be if I fell for every romantic cliché in the book? Should I give away the key to my proverbial chastity belt to every idiot who appeared on my doorstep bearing puppies? That gets a woman nowhere in this world.

A few days later, I got his response. He was trying harder, it seemed, but the poor dolt still hadn't gotten it right. Yes, I appreciated his tenacity, not to mention the presentation and practicality of the package. He'd taken the time to line the box with plastic, so it wouldn't ooze in the mail. How thoughtful. The ribbon was sloppily tied, but it was a nice touch. And the sloppiness was understandable in this case.

But again, the cliché! "I only have eyes for you!" Yes, yes, I got the pun. But the sad greying little orbs of jelly looked like they'd been gouged out of his head with a rusty spoon! If you can't take the time to do something right, for pete's sake, don't bother! I never cared for the color anyway: a shade of pale blue that reminded one of the sky on an over-cast day. And I resented all the implications that they were the exact shade of *my* eyes! How dare he be so presumptuous? We were not a perfect match at all, and his lack of imagination was terribly insulting. I told him so in the note I enclosed as I returned his latest gift. As a sudden afterthought, I called and repeated the note to his machine, realizing late that he'd be unable to read my graciously-written missive.

A few days went by. I almost missed him. I can admit it. A lady secretly enjoys every suitor, no matter how unwanted his attentions might be. Finally, his latest attempt arrived.

It was a bigger box than the others, but, then, it would have to be, wouldn't it? And when I opened it, tears leapt to my eyes.

No, not because of the gift. How could anyone be moved by such a thing? The latest cliché, the worst of them all! There was the plastic, again, and the ribbon, yes, thank you. But the message! Yes, how trite, you've given your heart to me. Thanks so much for nothing, Ronald. And no, I was not at all touched by his sacrifice. Love *is* sacrifice, of course, and it would appear that he finally understood that.

No, the realization that brought the tears was that Ronald could not have done this by himself. I'm a lady, and I can admit my shortcomings. I did not love Ronald. I found him dull, an uninspired romantic. But I couldn't help the pang of jealousy and wonder: who was the little slut who helped him?

Harry's Nebula

He'd lost last year, but just barely. Ellison, that cocky, talented, *prolific* bastard, came out of nowhere with that brilliant piece at the last minute. But this year was all Harry's. This year he'd nail it. "Jerusalem's Spire". Everyone who'd read it thought it was fabulous. "An instant classic in under ten thousand words," wrote one critic. A friend of his agent's told her that it had changed her life. There was no question of nomination.

Happy beyond words, Harry left his agent's office and rushed home to tell the Old Man.

The long black car in front of the house caused his heart to skip, his breathing shallowed, coming in gasps. Quickly, he fumbled in his pocket for his inhaler, taking a puff before finally putting the Saturn in park.

Expecting a team, he was surprised to find only the one man, Gates, in his severe black suit, like something out of those modern "hip" gangster films Harry so abhorred. Gates was sitting in the living room, on the couch next to the Old Man. They were waiting for him. Both faces were, on the surface, unreadable, but the over past year he'd come to know the Old Man very well. He seemed sad, sitting there, at a loss for what to say, but at the same time, he hoped that Harry would understand, and not make a scene. The large gray crystal eyes told Harry that and much more.

The Old Man raised one slender, five-fingered hand in greeting, and Harry's fingers gave out, dropping his briefcase in the hallway. He took in the scene and felt weak. Knowing it was coming, but almost unwilling to accept that it had come so soon.

"Hello, Harry," the Old Man said, but Harry didn't hear him. His eyes went to Gates, pleading as his legs moved him automatically into the living room.

"Not yet, please," Harry said, begging. "I'm not ready. I thought I would be, I really did. But it's too soon—"

Gates stood up, his face unchanged. "I'm sorry, Harry, but it's time."

"Just a few more days, please. A few days. Two days. What's two more days? It's been a year—"

"Harry," Gates said, as a warning. And Harry sank into a chair, defeated.

He felt the man's hand on his shoulder, a heavy hand, unfriendly, in spite of its intention. "You knew this was coming. He has other work to do."

"Yeah," Harry said, not looking up. Gates hesitated, then removed his hand.

"Let's go, Ambassador," he said.

The Old Man didn't move, his hairless head cocked to one side as it regarded the two men. "A moment, agent, if you please. To say goodbye?"

Gates froze, immobile, for a second, looking down at Harry, then at the Old Man. Perhaps it was his training, to gauge every situation as a potential hazard. "I'll be in the kitchen," he said at last, and left the two alone.

Neither spoke for a long time. The Old Man sat on the couch, watching Harry sit staring miserably at his feet. Finally, the Old Mad broke the silence.

"I enjoyed my time here with you, Harry," he said, in a voice of crystalline, of wind chimes in spring. Of gate hinges requesting oil.

Harry looked up at the Old Man, attempted a smile as his eyes welled with tears. "It isn't fair," he said. "It hasn't been a year."

"More than a year," the Old Man replied, eyes wide and unblinking. "But it was good time."

"I fell like there's so much more I could learn from you."

"Is that all?"

"No. Of course not. You know that."

He trailed off, losing the words as he stared at the Old Man, who had stood up, finally. His skin's delicate hue of blue-grey storm-morning sky began to ripple with deeper blues, deeper grays. As he spoke, his wind chime voice filled with heavier sounds, lead pipe rattling a basement, chain running through a lanyard.

"I don't suppose you'll be able to visit?" The Old Man asked.

"They won't tell me where they're taking you."

Another flutter, this time a marble grey with azure ribbons as the Old Man fought his emotions. "Then it's up to me," he said, forcing a smile. "I'll make them bring me back as I did before."

The hope managed to outweigh the doubt in Harry's mind. He thought back to when he found the Old Man, in the wreckage, up in the hills behind his cabin, where he'd gone to drink away his writer's block, do deny his newfound status of "divorced" and "unemployed". The last ditch effort to kick start a new career.

As he sat at the flimsy desk, in front of a silent typewriter and unopened bottle of whisky, there had been a flash outside, then an explosion that rattled the cabin windows. There were no skiers, not on his route, not at that time of year, so he alone made it to the crash, to the burning site of twisted metal that had gouged a furrow in the hillside and had melted the snow in a yard's diameter. Then he found the Old Man, who'd managed to crawl several feet from the destruction, bleeding a thick gray onto the ground.

Despite their respective odd appearances, neither seemed frightened by the other in the least. Soon the Old Man was unconscious, and Harry wrapped him in his outer coat and brought him back to the warmth and safety of the cabin. It had never once occurred to him that the Old Man might be dangerous. Fear was the farthest thing from his mind.

He'd gone on instinct, keeping the Old Man warm, wrapping him in blankets, bandaging the wounds, giving the Old Man water and soup. He had no way of knowing if this treatment would help or hurt. Would the soup be too much? Would the heat kill him? Harry had no way of knowing. The Old Man, though unconscious still, seemed to respond well to soft music, its color growing stronger.

In three days, he opened his eyes and spoke for the first time.

"Thank you for your attention," were the first words the Old Man said to him.

Harry was astonished for several seconds at the English. "Some of your people will be coming for me soon," the Old Man continued, wondering if Harry were mute.

Harry broke his own silence. "They know you're here?"

"The stop was unexpected. I got a little off course." The Old Man smiled, its thin face stretched tightly over bone. "But the trip had been arranged for some time."

Harry had no response; he could barely fathom the news.

"I am," the Old Man continued, feeling stronger, friendly. "What you might call an ambassador to your people. Some of my people are looking to settling down here. You could say I'm scouting out locations."

But Harry's "people" were slow in coming. So he provided the Old Man with more soup and more music. And the Old Man provided Harry with talk.

Great tales of warring races, quarreling beings who existed only as sound. Of twin suns rising over gaseous lakes. Of a pair of lovers who braved opposite ends of a glass desert, to be together in an oasis in the middle. The Old Man spoke of his time as the equivalent of a yeoman on a great interstellar battle cruiser, fighting pirates on the lip of a black hole. He told of his race's first contact with the others in the universe. Of the pioneers' first visit to Earth, before humans had climbed down from the trees. He told of a time when his race was welcomed here, when Harry's kind built landing strips for them at the top of tall brick structures. These were times before the invention of xenophobia.

And to all this, Harry listened. And later, while the Old Man slept, he would transcribe into a notebook, from memory, all that the Old Man said.

And when the men in identical dark suits finally arrived at the cabin door, Harry and the Old Man clasped each others' hands and bade each other farewell.

And a month later, publishers were clamoring at Harry's door.

He found that his material was limited, however, and stories of his own concoction sold for far less, and were less popular than those true stories the Old Man had told him. None the less, he was in high demand in the world when they had brought the Old Man back for a visit.

The Old Man had faked being sick, he explained to Harry, once the suits were gone and soup was on the stove. Claimed the walls of the institution were choking him. He would refuse to be studied, to impart information, threatened to break the treaty, promised the return of the abductions. ("Political activists," the Old Man explained. "Thought they could take hostages, trade for the ones your guys had of ours. All ended peacefully, but the media on both sides blew it out of proportion.") Finally, the suits had relented, and brought the Old Man to Harry, rather than vice versa.

Then the Old Man made his offer, out of the blue, without any urging what so ever from Harry: A cultural exchange. To stay with Harry for one year, to reward the man for saving the Old Man's life. And after the year was over, he'd work on whatever They needed. And after much grumbling, They relented, under the condition that the house be monitored, to ensure Harry would not injure their investment. And They made the Old Man promise not to reveal himself to anyone else. And they made Harry promise not to betray the Old Man to anyone. Both agreed to all stipulations.

Of course, Harry was elated. As soon as his roommate was established in the guest room, Harry went back to work, taking the Old Man's stories, translating and transcribing them into fictional terms. And the accolades poured in. He was publicly compared to Clarke and

Spinrad. Held up in print next to Heinlein, was grossing more than Asimov ever did.

Guilt came unbidden, sometimes staying for hours. But the Old Man seemed happy enough, enjoying Harry's film collection when he was writing, enjoying Harry's company when he was free.

The money, of course, was nice. The respect and the praise were the frosting, though. He declined all but the most prestigious events, in deference to his guest, he told himself, not wanting to leave the Old Man alone. Partly out of respect, partly out of fear of upsetting him, and partly out of a new anxiety he could not express. Much to his surprise, he began to feel sad when he wasn't with the blue-gray ancient, at a loss to explain it or define it. Not an overwhelming sadness, just a loss he couldn't ignore until he was back in the house, drinking coffee and talking again with the Old Man.

Though he had seen so much and was centuries older than Harry could even comprehend, the Old Man never made Harry feel insignificant or inferior in any way. He listened as closely to Harry's tales of a mediocre life as Harry did to the awe-inspiring spinnings of the outer worlds.

"You're as foreign to me as I am to you," the Old Man was fond of explaining. "What is mundane to you, I find to be fascinating candy."

But the year had ended, and now the suits had returned, and the Old Man was going away. And Harry felt life being ripped away.

"Can you ever forgive me?" Harry asked, his face wet with tears. And the Old Man flushed a royal blue, deeper than Harry had ever seen. Periwinkle swirling around the being's slender neck.

"Forgive you? For what, Harry? For saving my life?"

"I used you, Old Man. I stole your stories, passed them off as mine. Pretended that they came from me."

The Old Man looked astonished. "Harry," he began, and Harry dreaded the admonitions he was sure was coming. But the Old Man's color was steady, though still flushed. "You never stole anything from me," he said. "I gave those stories to you. In return for companionship, for friendship. You found a way to share them with others, that's all. And when I return to my friends and family, I'll share your stories with them."

"What could you tell?"

"A million things! You've seen mountains, Harry. Deer. You've gone scuba diving under a blue ocean and a golden sun. You've raised flowers from buds. Skied down a slope, in snow thick enough to hide in, trees rushing past you at thirty miles an hour. That's stuff I've never done. Stuff no one I know has ever done. I plan to use you for every bit you're worth, and Harry, you're worth it all."

Harry looked into the beautiful crystal eyes, at the smooth hairless head, earless, noseless, flowing spindly limbs, all a deep ocean blue. He coughed out a laugh. "You give me way too much credit," he said.

The Old Man's eyes looked directly at him, his color steady, nothing flowing. "You're my best friend, Harry. If we never see each other again, you will be my best friend. I'm going to arrange it so I can come back. And they'll let me, if they know what's good for them. They won't risk a war by denying me soup and a conversation. Think any of them can hold my attention? They would rather have chemical compounds and star cartography, and what does it mean if I turn sky blue?"

"It means you're irritated."

The Old Man smiled. "I spend a lot of time sky blue around them."

"I'm gonna miss you, Old Man."

"One last story?"

"Wait 'til your next visit," Harry said, wiping his eyes with the heel of his hand.

"I got a real good one. It's about two friends trying to avoid the rest of the universe."

"I think that's one of mine."

"Good luck with the award."

Gates returned to the room as Harry was saying, "Thanks." The Old Man's body flushed the color of wrought iron, it was the first time Harry had ever seen that color. "You waited a whole year!" The Old Man shouted at the suit in the doorway. "Give me two more minutes!" And Gates took at step back into the hall.

The two friends looked at one another, regarding each other as they had that first time the Old Man had opened his eyes in Harry's cabin.

Then the pair clasped hands, and then, for the first time ever, they embraced. The Old Man's arms long, wrapping around Harry's thick trunk; Harry's short arms wrapped around the Old Man's thin back, his color shifting beneath Harry's touch.

A moment later, a salute, a return, then the black car was gone from Harry's driveway. A lump in his throat remained, as well as a space in his heart where someone he called the Old Man would always be.

The Sponged Stone –
Or the Hunt for Christmas Yet-To-Come

Marley was dead: to begin with. Dead as a doornail for, by my calendar, over 153 years. But as for old Ebenezer Scrooge, famed gentleman of countless versions of the Dickens' tale, it would seem that he was not. Far from dead, the famous former-miser was sitting across from me in my booth at Shain's, looking very small, very tired, but most alive, and didn't look his age at all.

Not as robust as George C. Scott, though not as wizened as Alistair Sim—and the anthropomorphic opposite of *Uncle Scrooge McDuck*—Mr. Ebenezer Scrooge was a middle-sized, healthy chap, with a rosy glow to his cheeks and nose, due partly to having just come in from the cold and still awaiting his cup of Shain's infamous river-bottom coffee. Having removed and hung up his heavy black overcoat and oddly appropriate silk top hat, Scrooge sat before me, green silk vest upon white silk shirt, single gold ring on left ring finger, and a gleam in his sad pale blue eyes. His face was wrinkled, sagging slightly, looking barely a day over seventy—a complement considering that the gentleman was fast approaching his second century.

In seconds, his coffee arrived, delivered by Shain himself, who smiled at both the old man and me, then left us to our business at hand. Scrooge lifted the chipped cup to his lips, sipped, grimaced, then looked at me with a solemn face. "Mr. Shain tells me that you can help me, Mr. Taz," he said in a surprisingly husky voice. "I would be most grateful to you if you could. There have been many rumored to specialize in unusual cases such as mine, but as you can well understand, they usually turn out to be. . ." he paused for the right word. I took the opportunity to provide it.

"—Humbugs?" I said.

He smiled. "Precisely." With a slip of the mind, Scrooge took another sip of Shain's ghastly concoction, nearly gagging as it slid down his throat of its own volition.

"Terrible thing to do to innocent coffee beans, isn't it?" I asked, sipping my hot chocolate, my experience-proscribed beverage of choice. Scrooge nodded grimly, glaring at the thick black liquid virtually burbling in his cup.

"Has Shain provided you with the details of my predicament?"

"Not as such, Mr. Scrooge, no." What Shain had done was call me at home, interrupting my umpteenth viewing of *It's a Wonderful Life* with the inquiry "Would you like to meet *the* Ebenezer Scrooge?" Now in my past, I have never once heard of Shain playing Christmas Eve Fools jokes on his friends, and knowing all too well that he only calls with serious business, I ventured out into the lightly falling snow, avoiding main roads choked with last-minute shoppers, and hopped down to his diner, to see just what Shain was going on about.

Scrooge laced his time-gnarled fingers together and leveled his gaze at me. "Well," he began, "without boring you, I trust you've read the story?"

I nodded. "In complete and abridged versions, seen every major film version, and know the *Family Ties* and *Animaniacs* episodes off by heart."

Scrooge winced at the reminder. I guess if my life story had been remade a million times, not to mention parodied, and run back-to-back once a year for a hundred years, I'd be a little sick too. "Well, then you know how it ends. Before the sweetness and light, happily ever after part."

"What specifically?"

"When I turn to Christmas Future and say something like 'Let me sponge away the writing on this stone', or whatever damned fool thing I said."

"Okay."

"Well, when I said that, apparently, I sponged the writing away so completely . . ." he trailed off and splayed his hands.

"So completely you're still alive." I said, stating the obvious for our slower readers.

"Exactly," he said. "The spirits have forgotten about me. Moved on to bigger challenges, I suppose. Like trying to convert Bill Gates or Frank Cowett or something."

"So you want me to try to contact the Christmas Spirits?"

"Just the last one," Scrooge said. "He's probably the only one likely to be of much help."

I thought about this, not entirely sure how to go about doing any of it. But, without any other plans, I was perfectly willing to give it a shot, and said so.

"Thank you, Mr. Taz," Scrooge said. "It would be the perfect Christmas present to a very old man."

Which was, I guess, good enough for me.

And so it came to pass that Caesar Augustus published a decree that had nothing to do with my sitting in my loft on Christmas Eve with Ebenezer Scrooge, thumbing though an ancient book of incantations, trying to figure out how to summon the Ghost Of Christmas Yet-To-Come. As I did so, Scrooge sat warming his ancient bones by my roaring fire—which, as I had just built it, was not yet roaring, rather it was more like muttering irritably.

"Do you know how Dickens came to write *A Christmas Carol?*" Scrooge asked.

I looked up from my book, marking my place with my index finger. "No," I said. "And to be honest, I have been sort of wondering. Seeing as it's obviously a true story and all."

"I gave him my story as a Christmas present," he said. "I even gave him some of the money to publish it. He was in the middle of writing installments of *Martin Chuzzlewit*—he was having what he called "The Chuzzlewit agonies", because they weren't selling all that well."

Having read *Martin Chuzzlewit*, I wasn't a bit surprised.

"So on the first time I'd met Charles, we were at a Christmas party at an inn—*The Cock and Bull*, or some damned place—and he told me about all the trouble he was having. Debt up to his eyeballs. So I told him my story, to cheer him up, to tell him that money wasn't everything. He liked it so much, he asked if he could write it down. He was going to give editions as presents to his family. I gave him my blessings, even gave him some money for the printing costs." Scrooge gazed into the fire as he remembered. "Blasted thing has plagued me ever since."

I went back to my book. After a while, my eyes grew tired from reading by little more than firelight and, having no luck anyway, laid the book aside and rubbed my temples. "So, Mr. Scrooge," I began.

"Ebenezer, please."

"Alright. So tell me, Ebenezer, what have you done with yourself all this time?"

"Oh, this and that. Just trying to make people happy, yet keep myself out of the poorhouse. You have no idea how many leeches come out of the woodwork for a handout when they find out that you'll no longer have them arrested for trespassing. Almost went completely broke a couple of times in the beginning."

"I can imagine."

Scrooge grunted. "And when it became obvious that my life span had well surpassed that of "Normal", I thought that I was doubly blessed, and decided to redouble my generous efforts. Making investments that would ensure my purse would always be full should charity call upon me. I became the chief investor in hundreds of companies," he narrowed his gaze and smiled shrewdly at me. "Ever heard of Disneyland?"

"Of course."

"You might not have."

I had to smile admiringly at this. Scrooge went on.

"So year after year, I've raked in my profits, donated to charities, bought orphanages, that sort of thing, changed my name every thirty years or so. Right now people know me as Alan J. Clapsaddle."

I thought about this for a minute. "Yuck," I decided.

Scrooge shrugged. "I'm not overly fond of it myself," he sighed. "But as fulfilling as this doing unto others is, I have to say, quite frankly, that I've gotten too old for this sort of thing." He quickly glanced around. "Don't get me wrong. Giving is good. Really. But I've seen over four lifetimes here on Earth. Over one hundred and ninety

Christmases come and gone. Things get better, things get worse. I'd like to pass the torch."

"Do you have children?" I asked. "Grandchildren?"

He nodded. "And dozens of great-grandchildren. All dead." He added. "I've outlived everybody. It is now my turn."

"Wow," I said. And went back to my book. At the end of it, it was suddenly very clear to me, that even in the oldest of Harketanian grimoires, there probably isn't a passage useful for specifically invoking the Ghost of Christmas Future. I realized, with a sigh, that I'd have to start at the beginning. And I'd need help from true professionals. Easier said than done, as it was Christmas Eve and even professional witches tend to take the holidays off.

Regina Delamorte was not, thank God, her real name. But, as a witch's moniker, it was an eye-catcher. But it was hell trying to run her down. Her answering machine wished me Happy Holidays and told me to call back on Tuesday. Her car phone rang for an eternity. Her brother assured me that she was not at his place, and her mother wouldn't tell me anything at all. I finally found her. At Marshall Marshall's Christmas party. An event I was supposed to be attending, which, in the wake of all this Scrooge business, I'd forgotten about.

I apologized to Marshall, who, in his partially saturated state, not only couldn't care less that I wasn't there, was apparently unaware of my absence; he went and fetched Gina, who was none too happy to have her rejoicing and Noel-ing interrupted.

I explained the situation to her.

There was a long pause on the other end of the phone. I suspected a season-inspired insult pending. "Taz," she began. "You've been hitting the eggnog a bit hard tonight, haven't you?"

Do I know my colleagues or what?

"Gina, do you think you can slip away for a minute?"

"Taz, there is no way in Hell I am leaving this party. It's bad enough you've forced me to give my spot under the mistletoe."

"I'm not asking you to leave the party. Can you slip into the bedroom or the bathroom for ten minutes? I need you to try and find that ghost for me."

"The Ghost of Christmas Future?"

"Right."

"The one that looks like a low-rent version of the grim reaper?"

"Usually, though it depends on what film you're watching."

"You want me to post-pone my regaling so that you can play Ebenezer Scrooge?"

"This is *for* Ebenezer Scrooge. Try to pay attention, will you?"

There was another long pause. I tried to speed her up with "Can you just humor me, please?"

I was answered with: "You're gonna owe me big for this."

"Wait 'til you see what I got you for Christmas," I replied, making a mental note to rush out as soon as the stores opened on Tuesday. "Call me at my place as soon as you can whether you've located it or not."

I hung up and clapped my hands together, turning to my guest. "Well," I began. "Gina's going to try to cut to the chase. She's a more experienced summoner than I am. In the mean time, we're going to go a different route."

"What do you have in mind?" Scrooge asked.

"Well, just in case he's busy, I'm going to give Marly a shot."

Scrooge stared at me. "Marly? Why? What does Marly have to do with this?"

I shrugged. "He knew what was going on last time, didn't he?"

"I suppose."

"Well it's better than sitting around watching *Miracle on 34th Street* waiting for Gina to call."

"No it isn't."

"Richard Attenborough version," I replied.

"I wonder how old Jacob is doing." said Scrooge.

Jacob Marley was still in chains when I found him, though they had decreased to the size of paper clips and didn't look nearly as cumbersome. He was still a frightful sight, and looked shockingly like Sir Alec Guinness from *Scrooge*, right down to the kerchief tied around his head to keep his jaw from flopping open. He stood hovering in the center of the room, a bluish mist barely remaining in man-form, glinting slightly in the firelight. Through him, I could see my Christmas tree and its irregularly blinking lights.

"Scrooge," he moaned, the air rushing through him like a wind through a tunnel. "*Scroooooge*."

"H-hello, Jacob," Scrooge said, forcing a smile. "How have you been?"

Marley grinned. "Can't complain." He crossed his legs and sat in mid-air.

"Your burden has lessened, I see."

"Oh, yes. Not as heavy, though I miss the clanking and rattling."

"You do?"

"Mmmhmm. I used to do some part-time haunting when they were really impressive. Now all they're good for are slightly eerie windchimes around Halloween," He rested chin in palm and elbow on transparent knee. "So," he said. "How's by you?"

"Not bad, Jacob."

"How's the family?"

"Dead, thanks."

Marley blinked. "Dead? Say, how long's it been anyway?"

"About a hundred and forty-nine years," Scrooge replied. "Give or take."

"Good Heavens!" Marley exclaimed. "And you're still here. Or rather *there*? On Earth?"

"I'm afraid so."

"How can this be? Do the spirits know about this?"

"That's what we called you to find out," I said. Marley swiveled his head and stared at me, bug-eyed.

"Who the devil are you?"

"Uh, Jefferson Taz. Your summoner."

"Oh. Well, that would explain the pentagram I'm standing over." He said, more to himself, I suppose.

"Yes, it would."

"You know," Marley said. "I've never been summoned before. I wasn't even aware that that was what was happening."

"It is occasionally a subtle process," I agreed, though without much conviction having never undergone a summoning myself.

"Well, since I'm here, what can I do for you Ebenezer?"

"Well, Jacob, we called you to see if you had any idea, er, why I'm still alive."

Regretfully, Marley shook his head. "I'm afraid not, Ebenezer, no. The spirits don't keep much contact with me since you've changed your ways. Good change, too, Ebenezer. One-hundred-and-eighty degrees without quite altering your integrity. Quite a tightrope walk that. Why I've seen men change their ways only to get stepped on for the rest of their lives, but not you," Marley paused, seeing the puzzled look on Scrooge's face. "Oh, I kept an eye on you for a time afterward. Just to make sure you didn't get out of hand."

"Er, thank you, Jacob."

"Think nothing of it, Ebenezer."

"Um, not to be a Grinch, fellas. But we really should get going here. Christmas Eve is dwindling and I've got family to visit tomorrow."

"My apologies, Taz," Scrooge said. "Jacob, would you know where Future might be?"

Marley thought for a second, pressing the tip of his index finger to his temple and cocking his head, still hovering over the floor. "Hmmm. No, can't say as I do, Ebenezer. But if I run into him, I'll be sure to let him know you're looking for him."

"Er, is there much chance you'll be running into him soon, Jacob?"

"Uh, not really, no. Sorry, Ebenezer. We don't really travel in the same circles. But you never can tell. But I'll keep an eye out. I'll tell you what though, he's usually best reached around the time when the clock strikes three, remember?"

"All too vividly. And when it strikes four, he turns into a bed post."

Marley blinked. "Does he really?"

"He did last time."

"Well that's certainly a neat trick. Next time I see him, I'll have to get him to teach it too me." Marley began to fade away, waving as he did so. "My time is done. Merry Christmas, Ebenezer. Merry Christmas you odd looking young man."

"Merry Christmas, Jacob."

I grunted.

"And a Happyyy Newwww Yearrrrrr."

Scrooge sighed when Marley was gone. "Well, that was uneventful," he said.

"And melodramatic towards the end," I added with a hint of disgust. "He really should get with the times. Ghosts don't moan anymore. They just fiddle with your appliances, and blank out your e-mail." I glanced up at the clock. Five minutes to two am. Boy, this had been a long night already. Legally, it was Christmas Day. At least it was following the time-line of the story. "Two am is Christmas Present's allotted time, isn't it?"

"Last time I checked," said Scrooge.

Just to make sure, I flipped on the tube. On one of the local channels, the Henry Winkler version was playing. They were still in Christmas Past. "Now *she* was a dull spirit," said Scrooge.

"Who?" I said.

"Past. No sense of humor at all."

At two am exactly, my phone rang. It was Gina. "I got something," she said, though I'm not sure if he's who you're looking for. He's the hit of the party, though. Brought all his own food. Filled the room. Here, I'll put him on."

Though she was a bit sloshed, I had a hunch I knew who she was talking about. In seconds a deep voice was booming in my ear over the phone. "Come in and know me better, Man! Or should I say, come *over*. The party's just getting started."

"No prior commitments this year I see."

"Who is it?" said Scrooge at my elbow. I punched the speaker button on my phone and the room flooded with the cross-town voice of the Spirit of Christmas Present.

"Nothing that cannot wait until the wine is drunk and all are Merry!" said the voice, with a slight slur in its earth-shaking voice.

"Without keeping you from anything, Spirit," I said, shouting slightly so as to be heard over the rap version of "Silent Night" flooding the speakers in the background. "Would you happen to know where your third party is?"

"Christmas Yet-to-Come you mean?"

"That's the one. Any idea where he might be lurking."

"Absolutely! Are you sure you wouldn't rather join us, Man? The cornucopia overflowing."

"Thanks just the same, but I really have to find Future."

"That killjoy!" came the contemptuous equivalent of a thunderous mutter. "Yes, he's out and about, showing the wicked their individual fates. Not much trick in that: take them to a church yard, point at a tombstone. No real flair. No fun. He's always like that. Work, work, work."

"I agree. He should relax. Now, where might he be?"

"Try 112 South Graham Street. Apartment C," said Present. "Unless he's already turned into a bedpost there—" I shot a glance at Scrooge. "—In which case he's at 417 East Carson. Number 8. After that, I'm not sure. He sure as hell won't be here, I can tell you that! Oh, never. He's much too good for the likes of us."

"Thanks very much, Spirit. Put Gina back on." As he handed the phone over, I heard Marshall's distinctive air-raid siren doorbell. And immediately followed: "Come in and know me better, Man!" I shook my head to clear out the ringing churchbells. "Gina! I really owe you one!"

"Don't worry about it, Taz," she sloshed. "Th' guy's a ton of laughs. Even brought *Pictionary* with him." She laughed uproariously at this. I could tell that Miss Delamorte was just chock *full* of Christmas Cheer.

"Well, thanks anyway. Wish Marshall a Merry Christmas, or a Happy Hanukkah, or whatever faith he is this week."

I hung up. Grabbed Scrooge and together we raced out into the gently falling snow.

At this time, the gently falling snow was falling less than gently. The sky was white with the Cold Miser's latest tantrum. Jack Frost was wreaking havoc, almost literally seizing my nose with both fists. At this point, I should explain that the heater in my modest little economy car is a little fussy. It doesn't like the cold. The easiest way to heat up my car is to get in, let it run for a little while, then drive someplace warm.

My road gets excellent plow service. Due to this excellent plow service, it took ten minutes to dig my car out of the solid snowbank that had formed around it. And by the time we were out, and had done a few three-sixties on the side-road shortcuts, we arrived too late 312 South Graham. All we found there was a tall skinny guy running through the streets without a coat wishing every fire hydrant and adult theater a Merry Christmas.

So I threw my humble car into gear—pissing it off royally in the process—and we sped off, laughing all the way, to 317 E. Carson. Number 8.

Panting, sliding and slipping, Scrooge and I ran as fast as we could through the deep snow, trying desperately to prevent our bare skin from coming in contact with the metal railing as we hurried up the icy steps to the apartment building. We got to the door, after a moment of panic, we found the appropriate buzzer and pressed it.

We waited.

Scrooge stabbed a crooked finger at the buzzer again. We waited some more. Just as we were about to take a flying leap through the glass, a timid little voice came over the box. "Y-yes? Who's there?"

"Mr.—" (I found the name). "Garnet?" I said. "There's no time to explain. Is there somebody in there with you?"

There was a pause that seemed to last until Groundhog's Day. "Er, sort of. Sort of somebody."

"Please let us in. We have to see him."

"Don't let him turn into a hatrack or anything until we get there."

"Oh. Okay."

The buzzer sounded; we threw open the door and raced inside. Being an old, tired man who'd waited a long time for this moment, Scrooge beat me up the stairs by a full flight and a half, leaving me panting and winded on the sixth floor. Wheezing, I dragged myself into Number 8 by my fingertips. Garnet, a thin, nervous looking man held the door for me. "Jefferson Taz," I hissed, and looked around for Scrooge.

I saw him for just a minute. I swear, I think it was a minute exactly. Scrooge was standing, cane and hat in hand, before the tallest, most solid looking apparition I'd ever seen. It was exactly as the story had described right down to the skeletal hands: an ash-grey shroud covering darkness, a pool of half-glimpsed light worn as a curtain. It towered over Scrooge, who clutched its hem. Behind him, a headstone had materialized, with EBENEZER SCROOGE etched into its surface. The writing, it seem, was unsponged.

There were tears in Scrooge's eyes as he pressed the Spirit's hem to his cheek. With a sob, he looked over his shoulder at me and smiled. "Thank you, Mr. Taz. Thank you so very much."

"Merry Christmas, Mr. Scrooge," I replied.

"Merry Christmas."

And with that, the Spirit of Christmas Yet-To-Come and Ebenezer Scrooge vanished entirely from the living room of Mr. Henry Garnet.

When we were alone at last, without a headstone containing *anyone's* name, Henry Garnet turned to me. "Merry Christmas," he said, without knowing anything else to say.

"Merry Christmas," I returned.

"Was that *the* Ebenezer Scrooge?" He asked in a small voice.

"Yep."

"Oh."

We stood there for a moment. Two strangers on a very early Christmas Day. "They did it one night," Garnet said after a while. "They did it all."

I nodded. What else could I say. "Well, good night," I said and turned to go.

"Wait," he said. I turned back. "Just a second." He went to the couch. Next to the couch was an open window. Beneath the window was East Carson St., which was the main thoroughfare for this end of town. "Here," he said as he turned back. In his hand was a semi-automatic rifle, complete with a sight. He handed it to me, stock and all. "I hadn't loaded it yet. I was going to do that tonight. Before they came." He smiled. There were tears in his eyes. "I don't have to now. I never had to really." He shrugged. "Well, good night. Merry Christmas," He said as he closed the door behind me.

I stood in the hallway of Garnet's building, looking down at the rifle I held in both hands. The spirits had done it in one night, I saw. I felt like I had been given a gift too.

Scrimshaw

She waited a year, just as DeGris had asked, but the hate was still there. She'd tried to let it go, to get on with her life; she went back to work, resumed her routine, but Robert's face was always there when she closed her eyes, leering over her, telling her in his rough, smoky voice, that she wanted it this way. With eyes open, she'd see him now and then on the street and immediately cross before he saw her, or duck into some shop to avoid him. It didn't happen often, and her terror was long since swallowed by the hate.

She wanted him dead.

No, that wasn't true. What she wanted was for Robert Etienne to feel everything he'd forced upon her: the humiliation, the pain, the terror that lingered like a white-hot knot in her belly. To go through the utter and complete degradation, the self-loathing, the emptiness. To feel the stares as he walked through the streets, the look of disgust or pity in the eyes of everyone he met for the rest of his life, as they recognized his face from the papers, or just *knew*.

She remembered how she'd found him: an unfamiliar bar on a cool and lonely October night. A series of lonely nights were made less lonely by his charming smile. Until one night when she found him with his friends, and they'd had too many drinks and too much anger and too much time.

Josephine DeGris was the first person she'd run to after it happened. And it was DeGris who held her hand, took her to the doctor. But in her rage and terror and humiliation, she'd already been home and bathed, to wash the feel of their hands from her body. So the hours' worth of tests yielded very little, the medical prodding, the clinical questions regarding her health, her cycle, her hygiene. DeGris was there during the statements to the police, during the snickers from the back rooms when they thought she wasn't looking. Afterward, there were weeks of sideways glances from men on the street—how could they know?—looks containing the words "slut" and "whore" in equal doses.

And DeGris sympathized, consoled, counseled, whispered, and told her to wait until after the trial. So she sat at the table beside her lawyer, while the courtroom filled with Robert's friends and drinking buddies: his lawyer, the witnesses, the jury, the judge. He was a lifetime local boy, just out to have some fun and things got out of hand. It was a summed-up phrase which drowned out her screams at night. And DeGris had asked her to wait yet again. A year, this time, to sweat out the poison.

The year passed and the poison welled up inside her. Sixty days and Robert was free, time served, conscience clear, and she became a running dog, it seemed. He didn't pursue her or make any attempt at all to find her. Or apologize. Or gloat. But she felt his eyes on her anyway, in the glances of other men who somehow knew.

October came again. And Pamela returned to DeGris with her request.

"I considered moving," Pamela said, sipping DeGris' sassafras tea, sitting in a comfortable, stiff-backed chair with its hand-embroidered cover. DeGris was somewhere else in the room, tending to her pottery by the sunny window, hidden by the vines and spider plants which grew in abundance, hanging from the ceiling, fronds spilling out across the floor. DeGris was never still, unless she was holding Pamela, stroking her hair to stop her crying. Only then did her hands stop fine tuning her world.

"I wanted to leave and never come back," Pam continued. "But I felt marked. I felt like everyone in the entire world already knew. So what was the point?"

Josephine's hands closed around the spinning lump of clay on her wheel, smoothing it out into a new pot. She could see the pot in the formless clay, so she was bringing it out, which is what it wanted. "There was another reason, yes? You didn't want to leave because this is your home. You grew up here, too. Why should you leave? What did you do wrong?"

Pam, this time, was silent.

"I already heard you nod, Pamela," Josephine said, her chocolate-colored hands caked with terra-cotta. "But that *is* your feeling, yes? You want Robert Etienne to go away. Eh? Or something worse? Still? After a whole year?"

"You know what I want, Josephine."

It always felt odd to call such a familiar friend by such a long formal name. Though she liked being called Pam, Josephine only called her Pamela, and Josephine would only be called Josephine. Acquaintances and business relations called her DeGris.

"You want revenge, Pamela, and that is all. There's hate in your heart for this man. What about the other two? Eh? You hate them as well and equally? Or only Etienne?"

Pamela flinched, thinking of the other sets of hands, the other pair of grinning, mad, drooling faces, their mouths on her. "I hate Robert more. He pretended to be a friend, then acted like I was some kind of animal. Worse. He threw me away like garbage."

"He is a man, Pamela. No better. Little should be expected from them."

"And that's an excuse? Let men act like men? That excuses what he did to me? For destroying my life?"

Josephine closed her fingers around the narrow part of the pot, narrowing it further. It wanted to become a vase, aspiring beyond its pot beginnings. The quiet whir of the wheel's motor blended in with the soft and constant hiss of the ceiling fan.

It was hot in the room. Moist, from the plants and the uncharacteristic humidity of the new autumn. The windows, though open, were sweating. Pam finished her tea and set the cup down on a small wooden table beside her, its edges and legs covered with carvings and ornate patterns, smoothed and finished. The hot tea had cooled her body and allowed her to fend off the smothering heat.

"You know what I want, Josephine," she said again. "He never paid for what he did to me. He got a slap on the wrist!" Her hate was welling up now, spilling out as anger tinged with rage. Her breathing became erratic. "Sixty days for simple assault! He broke my nose! I had a ruptured uterus! I may never have children, Josephine! My lawyer never even let me take the stand!"

"I know what happened, Pamela."

"Then you should understand!"

"No, girl, *you* should understand. You need to understand what you are asking me to do. What you want done to another human being - and that is what he is, like it or not. Robert Etienne deserves to be beaten for his crimes. But let me ask you this, and think about your answer: Are you the only woman who has ever been raped?"

Pamela stood up. Her hands were shaking as she walked to the back of the room, and pushed aside the vines hiding Josephine from view. DeGris was concentrating on her vase, the wheel turning around and around, and the clay, now formed, sliding between her wet hands. She glanced up, but did not stop. Pamela took a deep breath before she spoke, her voice even, her green eyes narrow and flashing.

"What I wish upon Robert Etienne, I wish upon every man has or who will ever raise a hand to a woman."

Josephine didn't falter, her thumbs molding the lip of the vase. "Some might say the woman deserved it."

Pamela's lip twitched, her voice filled with emotion. "Men say that."

The soft whir stopped, the silence filled the room to the corners. Josephine took her foot from the pedal and swiveled around on her stool.

"I have already done what you asked," she said, neither happy, nor resentful. She said it simply, a declaration of fact. And Pamela's heart jumped at the news.

She used to love this time of year. Especially as a child. October magic, creeping in, hiding around the corner of the last day of September, building until Halloween. Years later, she'd outgrown the simple joys of dressing in costumes, preferring to don the more subtle, invisible masks of adulthood. But watching the young ones running under the streetlights, their plastic capes flapping behind, she felt a little chill from the electric October magic. One year ago, October magic left

Pam's life forever. It sounded melodramatic even to her, but it was true. Magic was no longer something she believed in.

She knew he'd be there, just as she'd found him the first time, playing pool with his friends. It was long after last call, but Eli owned the bar, and after-hours was Robert's special time with his buddies. She couldn't have planned it better. Brandon and Eli were both in there with him, and no one else. That late, there were few people on the streets. It took no effort to secrete Josephine's gift in the alley in the back.

She stood outside and watched him through the window for a bit. The bar was dim, the jukebox playing some unfamiliar twangy tune. He was smiling his broad smile, joking with Brandon as he bent over the pool table to make a shot, his muscles moving under his T-shirt and tight blue jeans. He still had the pretty-boy model look: cleft chin, sandy brown hair, bright brown eyes with life behind them. The pool cue slid easily through his strong rough hands; she could remember when they first met, how she'd longed to feel those hands on her skin. And then she remembered what they actually felt like when he finally touched her. Like cactus needles. There was a beer bottle on the table, near the corner pocket at his elbow. She remembered the feel of one similar. Like a cold fist.

A shudder ran through her, a frosty wind, though the air was a hot wet blanket. Nothing moved on the street, shining under the streetlights. As the jukebox song died away and stillness filled the gap in the air, she forced a smile and tapped her nails against the glass, her hand hidden by the 'closed' sign hung on their side. The soft clicking cicada noise penetrated their laughter, caught their attention as all three looked her way. Eli jumped. Brandon stared dumbly.

Robert smiled as if she were the only thing he'd ever wanted to see. His grin grew rats in her heart, but she commanded her own smile to freeze, and Brandon was sent over to let her in.

"Hey, Pam," Brandon mumbled, not looking at her, studying his shoes. She gave him the present of a glance he barely saw and walked past him. Behind the bar, Eli's eyes spilled poison in her direction, but she paid him no mind. Robert's gaze drank her in and he let out a low whistle, shamelessly, as she walked. She heard, but did not see, Brandon lock the door behind her.

"Jesus, God, Pam, you look beautiful," came Robert's compliment, riding the crest of the whistle.

And she did, too, on purpose. It took a few hours to get it right, making and re-making selections from her closet, of the nighttime clothes she hadn't worn in a year. Ultimately, it was the thin, sheer green silk blouse, alternately tight and breezy in all the right places; the tightest leather skirt she could walk in; the highest heels to show off her long legs. Dangling silver earrings were symmetry on either side of heavy makeup and short-cropped, sprayed up brown hair. She carried a single, tasteful handbag, and inside was a simple, nickel-plated .38 revolver.

"Hello, Robert," she said, a tinge breathlessly, with anticipation his ego would no doubt mis-read.

"I never thought I'd see you again," he said, a little sad and a lot surprised. "I thought you hated me. Us. All of us."

She smiled again, straight pins pierced her cheeks. "I do," she said. He jumped as if slapped. "More than you'll ever know. But I couldn't stay away."

Before he could reply, she backed up against the pool table, rested her behind on the ledge and slid up on her toes until she was seated on its edge. She did this all in one motion, never taking her eyes from his.

Another song began on the jukebox, a faster-beat, a steel-guitar rhythm.

"All I've thought about all year is seeing you again," she admitted. She hadn't lied yet.

"Hey, Bobby." It was Eli, coming around from behind the bar. "That bitch is up to something, man. Get her out of here." Eli had always hated her. Even when he was on top of her.

"Shut up, Eli," Robert said, not looking at the bar's owner. "Pam's an old friend, remember?"

"I know who the hell she is!"

"I remember you too, Eli," Pam said. "You too, Brandon. How are you, honey?" The question slit her tongue lengthwise, but caused the younger man to blush.

Planting her hands on the table, she leaned back, her eyes still on Robert's face, studying the structure, her heart racing. The suspense was such lovely agony. "Get me a beer, Robert. Please."

Blood rushed to his face at the 'please', and his breath came in an audible gasp. His smile turned goofy for a second, then he recovered with the coolness she'd grown accustomed to. "Anything you want, baby," he said.

Behind him, Eli watched uneasily, suspicious, nervous. "Bobby?" he said.

"Goddammit, Eli," Robert half-turned, eyes on fire. "Get her a beer!"

Stung, Eli jumped, scurried behind the bar. There was a small table fan back there, stirring what was left of his hair as he passed in front of it. He dug a bottle out of the cooler, bringing it to her, frosty cold. With reluctance, Eli offered the bottle. She reached for it, but Robert snatched it from him and handed it to her himself. She favored him with another vomit-inducing smile and took it. The cold glass felt good in her hands, the night was so hot. Robert's eyes remained on her face as she unscrewed the cap, touched the bottle to her lips for a moment before drinking.

Behind Robert, Eli was back against the bar, looking trapped. Brandon was motionless beside the door. It didn't matter that they were there or not. As far as Robert was concerned, there were only two people in that room.

"Robert," she whispered. "Pull the shades."

"Brandon, yank down those shades," he barked. And like a robot, Brandon did what he was told, drawing down the heavy shades, covering the large windows, eliminating the outside world.

Eli was sitting down, looking sick. "Hey, now, Bobby, come on—"

But Robert ignored him. He moved in to kiss her, but she put a hand to her lips. "This isn't love, Robert," she said. He stared at her, not comprehending, then the lights went on behind his eyes as her meaning sank in. He nodded and his hands went to his belt.

"I'm sorry what happened, Pam," he said, fumbling with his jeans. "I won't be rough this time, I promise."

There was a whisper as the denim fell to the floor.

"I will," she promised, and laughed, loud, unable to contain it any longer. Robert froze for an instant, unsure of the laugh, as the others were unsure. But her hand went to the top button of her blouse, and as a hint of skin emerged, she had him in her spell again. His arms went around her, undoing the clasp of her skirt, and her hand went to her side. It found the handbag beside her on the table, opening it with a flick of thumb and forefinger, sliding inside and coming out with the .38. Robert's slid his hand down and under her shirt, caressing her back. She put the cold metal barrel against his ear and said, "Shh. Don't move." And gave a low whistle of her own.

Hypnotized, the others didn't move, not even when the splintering crash came from the back of the bar. It was like a dream, Eli and Brandon slowly turned as Josephine's gift walked through the broken back door. Then their eyes registered confusion, incomprehension, then horror.

It was almost seven feet tall, and had taken Josephine over two months to construct it. She had to fire the pieces separately, for her kiln was far too small. It was man-like, but an impressionist's sculpture. Thick arms and legs and a trunk that could be called muscular, if indeed it were made of flesh and muscle, rather than rich, rough, unglazed red-brown clay. Its head was almost featureless, deep slits for eyes and a mouth, a jutting outcropping of rock served as a nose. It moved with the sound of a sealed crypt opening, clay grinding against clay, powder puffing out from its joints. But it was fluid—whatever gave it life also gave it grace. It came into the bar and Brandon began to moan.

Robert didn't dare turn his head, she was pressing the gun's barrel so hard against him, he was sure it would punch through his skull. He heard the heavy footsteps, heard Brandon's wounded-dog howl, heard Eli chattering "Uh-uh-uh-uh—" All behind him, where his eyes could not go, for which he was almost thankful.

Eli had crawled onto the bar and was scooting backwards down the length of it, anxious to get as far as possible from the creature. Brandon had sunk to his knees, still moaning, terrified beyond words. Josephine's gift moved quickly towards the pool table, stopping as it reached Brandon's side. Pam nodded and its head swiveled to look down at the young man, who was kneeling on the rough wood floor and had wet himself in terror. The statue's right arm ended in a lump of hard clay, serving as a fist. Its arm shot out, with a speed that frightened even Pam, and Brandon fell heavy to the floor, his face a bloody, shapeless mass of meat and bone. Blood pooled and began to spread across the floor.

The statue took two steps towards the pool table and stopped at a nod from Pam. That was all the communication the two needed. Josephine had trained it well.

Pam leaned back a bit and looked into Robert's panicking eyes. They were wide and vast. Pam's, however, were cold and hard, but she still couldn't help but smile. She opened her mouth to speak, but despite a well-rehearsed speech, she couldn't find any words. Her mouth closed with a snap and she slid out from under him, keeping the pistol against his temple. Once she was standing, free from his weight and his scent, the only sentence she found was: "This is for you, Robert."

And he finally found the strength to turn and look at Josephine's gift. His eyes widened further than he would have thought possible, if he were, indeed, capable of thought. He looked it up and down, the featureless, glowering face, the thick arms, the lumps of fist—no, only the right fist was a heavy boulder. The left hand had fingers, four, counting the thumb, and each one was the size of three of his. It was the left hand that was reaching out for him, as he opened his mouth to silently scream. The scream found voice after his eyes dipped down past the creature's waist.

Between the tree-trunk legs, a phallus stood out like a ramrod; it was the size of a broomstick, the length of Pam's forearm, rounded off. Though Pam had been disappointed it wasn't a sharpened stake, it would do nicely.

She repeated, "This is for you, Robert," as the statue's left hand closed around his neck and slammed his head forward, into the pool table.

Behind her, Eli was on his feet, screaming. "You bitch! You bitch! You—" She didn't care to listen any longer. Like a stranger in her own body, she raised the pistol and shot him. The bullet punched through him, half an inch below his heavy gut. Blood poured from the wound and from his mouth as he coughed up a gout. He collapsed to the floor, breathing heavily and twitching. She turned away from his death-throws, it didn't interest her. She wanted to watch Robert.

He was screaming, of course, his hands thrust out in front of him, frantically grasping for—she wasn't sure if he knew. Some comforting hand hold, something familiar to take him back to reality. Josephine's gift had him pinned to the table, it's left hand holding him down. Blood was trickling from his broken nose, staining the table felt. It stood behind him, and already it had him impaled, its hips bucking back and forth, in time with Robert's screams. Blood was running down his legs, into his jeans and underwear.

Pam was aware that her hands were shaking; she fumbled with her handbag, dropping the gun to the floor, its clattering impact scaring her. She felt embarrassed, not as thrilled as she thought she'd be, watching

Robert's rape. She'd concocted an image of it, a fantasy, which she'd been playing in her head for a year. Her trembling fingers found her cigarettes and her plastic lighter. A recent vice. It took effort to hold the flame still enough to light. Robert's screams were disintegrating into meek whimpers, helpless pleas of "No more." But the gift wouldn't stop without a signal from her. And she wasn't about to give the signal. Not yet.

"Please. . . Pam . . . make it stop," Robert cried, tears and snot mixing with blood. His front teeth were missing. Pam amended that thought. They were there on the table in front of him, not missing at all.

Her foot was tapping without her realizing it, but she couldn't stop it. After another second, she spun around, not wanting to watch any longer. But behind her, her eyes found Eli, dead in a pool of blood in the corner, his eyes open and staring. The little fan behind the bar made another pass of the room, and a light breeze caressed her hair. Her eyes darted towards the door, found Brandon, looked away quickly.

Robert's cries were becoming weaker, and the statue had not broken its even rhythm. She whirled around and found her hate again, right where she'd left it. She gave a nod to the statue and it thrust forward, viciously. Robert's scream pierced the air; arms shot forward, fingers splayed in pain. Teeth set, she stalked over to him, seized his hair, forced him to look up at her with his watery eyes, blood smeared face.

"Say you understand! Say you understand why this happened!"

"I—I—" came the answer.

She yanked his hair until she felt some tear out. He gave a blubber in response. "Tell me, Robert! Tell me you know why I did this!"

"Because I raped you. . . I'm so sorry. I'm so sorry!"

"No! Not good enough! I begged you to stop! I begged you! I thought I . . ." She trailed off. Stared at a point on the table past his head. Remembering.

They'd taken her on the table, each one having a turn while the other two held her down. Tearing her clothes, slobbering on her, hitting her. It was Eli who'd used the bottle. Brandon who'd gone only once. Robert who told her how good she was doing, that it would be over soon.

The last memory made her slam his head forward, back onto the table. Once. Twice. "I hate you!" she shouted into his ear. He shrank from her. The cigarette slipped from her fingers as she stared down at him. She wanted to speak, to get hold of herself, pull herself together, give him the speech. That he couldn't hurt her anymore. That this was revenge. To make him understand what he'd done. But there were no words. Only a shriek, a howl of raw emotion, which came with her beating fists, wedging her shoulders between his and the statue. The onslaught lasted a second, then her legs gave out and she sank to the floor, crying herself, begging something inside her for some sort of release.

Robert's breath was coming in gulps, still impaled on the statue's shaft. Slowly, weakly, she glanced up. The gift was looking down, silently, at her. She gave a feeble nod and the statue backed away, accompanied by a sudden sharp cry from Robert, who lay across the table without moving. Bracing herself against the floor, she stood up awkwardly and moved away from him, retrieving the gun in one lumbering step.

Behind her, she could hear him sniffling, standing, pulling up his pants, redoing his belt. She wanted to ask him, bitterly, if he'd brag about this encounter with Pam-the-slut, but again, the words were missing. He stopped, swallowed hard. Then she heard him leave, walking quickly, with difficulty, through the broken back exit. She turned her head and saw a last blur of his departure, then she let herself fall forward a little, until her forehead touched the wall, and she stayed there until her own tears stopped, and she stopped panting, the breath coming out in a final sigh.

Turning, she saw the statue, looking at her. She noticed, suddenly, that its face did have one feature. Tiny etchings in the forehead. They could have been words, or simply designs, put there by Josephine's artistic license. She took a step forward, curious about the markings, when the creature suddenly collapsed, its parts crumbling, disintegrating into dust, until there was nothing on the floor but a pile of clay and dirt. It had been created for a single purpose, and, its mission complete, it was allowed to rest.

Somehow, the heat had broken that night. Autumn had finally arrived.

"You are done, then. Your goal has been met?" Josephine asked, through the narrow gap in the chained door. Outside, in the hall, Pam nodded. "Then it is all over? You can get back to your life?"

Again, she nodded. Her makeup was smeared with the track lines made from her tears. Josephine thrust her hand through the opening. "Give me the gun. I shall dispose of it."

Pam did as she was asked. "I thought I'd feel better," she said. "I thought it was what I wanted."

"Revenge is a man's game," Josephine said simply. It made Pam angry.

"You don't know what it's like!" she said. "It didn't happen to you!"

"Not this particular instance, no," Josephine said, and closed the door, leaving Pam alone in the hallway. She wanted to beat the door with her fists, get Josephine to open up and hold her, like she had every other time she'd needed her. But the artist was inside, and Pam was in the hall. And she felt all the more the prisoner. She thought again, as she walked down the dim hallway, that once it was all over, the hate would be gone. But it was still there, sketched onto bone, and etched into permanence after a year's worth of acid, a delicate, intricate web of complete hatred. It was hers, it seemed, for ever. To live with.

Next Thursday was Halloween. The leaves had finally begun to turn...

A Roof Above Our Heads

The house had teeth and eyes.

The shattered glass of the windows on the upper floor glared down at us, somehow holding back a shining blackness within. At the ground level was a smashed and jagged picture window, a toothy maw waiting to swallow us whole. It was a massive structure, and we stood at the very front, a yard away from the front steps leading up and in, while either end of the mansion stretched out and disappeared into the encircling woods of the hill.

It was sunrise on a chilly November morning, and a wind filled with straight pins whipped around us, slapping at us as we stood on the untidy lawn, at the top of the steep hill, looking up at the house that had been fashioned, brick by brick, by hands of pure hatred. Dead leaves swirled about, their dried corpses resurrected from their autumn passing. But nothing stirred inside the house. I'd be willing to bet that once inside, despite the absence of unbroken glass, the air would be calm and quiet.

"Feeling anything yet, Mr. Taz?"

I glanced over at Josek. He'd asked the question without looking at me, without tearing his singular gaze from the house. Besides myself and Josek, there were two other men, large men, in the yard with us. Hulking, strapping men, as strong and weathered as the house itself. Josek had introduced us briefly: the bald man was Ed; the black man, Isaac. Josek had referred to them as "contractors", and they stood leaning on sledgehammers, pick-axes slung carelessly over shoulders, waiting for the order to kill.

I took a deep breath and let it out slowly. The "contractors" exchanged smirks of a private joke, and I felt defensive anger begin to bubble up. But I exhaled and the anger vanished, and I let the house speak to me.

"The house did this to me," Josek said, removing his dark glasses, revealing his missing eye, the skin of his forehead on the left side melting down over the empty socket. The entire left side of his face was a mass of angry red and white scar tissue, rolling and rippling back around his head, like torn and wrinkled velum wrapped around an orange. It looked as if something had latched onto the side of his head and pulled until uneven layers had peeled away from his skull. If his story was to be believed, that was exactly what happened.

We sat in Shain's diner, my usual booth in the back corner, by the window overlooking the parking lot and the rolling hills beyond. This view was preferable than that of the highway afforded the front of the diner. I sat with my back against the wall, untouched Coke in front of me, watching beads of perspiration running down the glass, to avoid looking at the ruined face of the man across from me.

The information about my prospective client ticked across my mind's eye like a stock market banner: he was Darren Josek, fifty-one years old, investment broker from Chicago. Inherited a local mansion from a cousin five years ago. It was rumored that a great deal of valuable something or other was hidden somewhere in the house—in the walls, beneath the floorboards, in pipes or behind fireplace bricks. I yawned when he told me the story over the phone.

Same old song: get Jefferson Taz for a treasure hunt; let him use his "special talents" to find your missing fortune. I get calls like this about a dozen times a year. But then again, Shain put Josek onto me, and Shain's known me a long time; he knows to weed out the crazies. So I agreed to meet with my would-be fortune hunter and hear him out.

And then the man with the white-blond hair and half his face missing sat down across from me, and I found it impossible to look at him, yet impossible to really look away, catching myself glancing at him out of the corner of my eye, hypnotized almost beyond decorum by the criss-crossing highway of bas-relief scars. I've seen disfigurements of all kinds before, every imaginable form of visible disease, injury, decay. I've stared into inhuman faces, learned to do it with a smirk and a wink. Josek's scars were, really, no worse than the worst I'd seen. But there was the mad hatred burning in his single ice-blue eye that made me shudder.

"Been battling that goddamned house for five years," he continued. His voice was a metal blade scraping concrete. I wondered how far down his body the scars ran, how much had been torn away? With my peripheral vision, I traced the path down his face, seeing the scars vanish into the collar of his dark topcoat, the lapels flipped up and pinned at the throat with a garnet pin. His grating voice continued.

"My brother, Robert, put it there, the inheritance he stole from me. Two-and-one-half million dollars my grandfather made in the steel industry in the early thirties. Hidden somewhere in that vicious house.

"It killed Robert," he said, staring at me with that single burning eye. "Threw him down the stairs after years of torturing him. But he hid that money, I know it. I've seen it. With Robert out of the way, the house was mine, finally. Then it began by playing with me. Every time I'd get close to the money, it would move it somewhere else. It'd wait," he said, giving a small laugh. "I'd get a glimpse of the strong box hidden inside some hole I'd just knocked in, and then the wood would seal up and the box would vanish to some other part of its bowels," he coughed, chest hitching. He composed, took a sip of water, and continued. "And then it began to try to kill me. For five years, on and off, it tried to murder me, but I beat it every time. Until last year, when it did this." He needlessly gestured at his ruined face, the left side completely still, unmoving during the entire speech, without a twitch while he spoke.

"I spent five months in that hospital, connected to tubes and monitors. Plastic surgery is out of the question, too much is missing. Doctors hadn't expected me to live through the trauma and blood loss. Not the first time someone pronounced me a goner," he said, eye flashing with ego behind the hate.

It was almost a full minute before I realized that he was finished, and I was at a loss for words. What do you say after something like that? I could tell that there was truth behind the tale, the proof was sitting unblinking in the booth across from me.

I was tired. The last few months had royally kicked my ass, hard and repeatedly. Time had held me down while the events beat me up. But Josek's words took hold and I couldn't explain why. I looked up at him, forcing myself to meet his solid burning gaze. I didn't say a word. I simply nodded. And the nod was returned, the deal struck with a telepathic handshake. And then it was done.

Standing on the hill, listening to the building. I was mildly surprised—the house had nothing to say. Most houses—"clean" houses—have a residue of passive resonances, latent psychic energy imbedded in the structure by all its previous inhabitants. Creaks and groans common to any house, attributed to the all-encompassing explanation of "settling" were often the house's thoughts, memories, psychometric footprints that even a half-assed sensitive can detect. "A house is everyone who has ever lived there," was the most famous quote. (Anatole France? Huxley? I could never remember.) This house—which, from the outward appearance, should have been leaping into the air and shrieking obscenities—was utterly and terribly silent. This scared the shit out of me.

I glanced back at Josek and answered his question with a shake of my head, not wishing to convey my unease.

He smiled then, the parts of his face capable of smiling, and the effect was horrifying. It was the face of Mengele at Hanukkah, Dahmer at Thanksgiving. The smile told me of his planned revenge, to torture the house until it begged him to kill it. I could see the history behind this desire, how long he'd dreamed of this day, lying in a hospital room, staring up at the white ceiling, tubes and wires snaking out of his bandaged body.

We advanced up the creaking steps and were quickly swallowed whole.

By way of comparison, this house made Shirley Jackson's *Hill House* look like Cinderella's Castle. Inside, the darkness had texture, the gloom physical, coating the corners in thick layers, an opaque sheet wrapping itself around you, preventing you from moving freely, breathing comfortably. When you inhaled, you inhaled the darkness, the quiet. The house had spent many years embroidering itself with cobwebs of murk, breeding and nurturing claustrophobia in its walk-in womb.

I wish I were exaggerating. "Heh, heh, there's my whimsical sense of humor." Instead, I felt like the tongue-tied Lovecraftian narrator come face-to-face with the indescribable creature of dread. Except I was already inside the belly of the beast.

Above us, the lights flared from an ornate chandelier as Josek flipped on the power, but the illumination did little to chase away the gloom. Behind me, I heard him take a deep satisfied breath, and let it out. He came into view, arms spread wide, ready to take what was so rightfully his. "Start wherever you like, boys," Josek announced, turning to grin at me like a rotting jack-o-lantern. "Mr. Taz will warn us when the house wants to play."

I ignored the chuckling of the two interchangeable "contractors". "I'm going to have a look around," I said. "See if I can find the heart of your house."

"Good," he replied, flopping back into a plush leather chair, dust billowing up around him. "I want to rip it out with my bare hands."

As the contractors shouldered their tools of destruction, I turned on my heel and left the room, journeying down the dim hall as the sounds of grunts and the crunching of splintering wood grew faint behind me.

And then I was alone in the house. Josek's psychic watch-dog, in tune with his victim, there to alert him when and if the house wanted to fight back. I came to another doorway, which opened into another vast room. I flipped the wall switch as I entered, and watched the shadows slink away from the light, retreating to their comfortable corners, scuttling beneath sheet-covered furniture. I was alone now, in a room with wall-mounted pendulum clocks—one on each wall, each still and silent, the frozen faces each reading a different time.

It wasn't any old and forgotten house—that much was obvious. But was it the malevolent beast capable of throwing a man down the stairs, capable of torturing and tormenting a living human? Poltergeists were known for wreaking havoc, but there were very few documented cases of the living being actually harmed, much less killed, by poltergeist activity. So the question was, if Josek was telling the truth, if his insanity hadn't gotten the better of him, and his cousin *was* killed by and in the house, were we dealing with a poltergeist, or were we battling something else?

I remembered a line from Shirley Jackson's *The Haunting*—it was impossible not to think about that book, standing in a house such as this. 'Some houses are born bad,' was the line echoing through my head.

Beneath my feet was a thick carpet that would have been the color of red wine, were it not itself covered by a carpet of dust. There were no windows in this room, no link to the outside world. I was Schroedinger's cat; if the entrance and exit to the room were closed off, would I cease to exist to the outside world?

I took another breath and tried to reach the house again. It should have been an easy link, but the gloom had hold of me, the dread caught my chest in a vice grip. I was waffling between sympathy and terror--who was the victim here? Josek or the House? Or did they deserve to destroy each other? Why would anyone want to live in this furnished crypt? Why would anyone even build such a structure? It was an intricate Skinner Box whose sole purpose was to create shadows, a hatred factory, a maze infested with evil.

There was no link. The house remained utterly silent in my mind. It was speaking to me in other ways. I realized this now, thinking rationally, forcing the fear to subside. It was contacting the empath in me. I slowed my breathing, and, gradually, my racing heart followed suit. I forced myself to be calm again.

I heard another distant crash somewhere far behind me. How deep had I gone? I hadn't thought ahead far enough to unspool golden thread to lead me out of the labyrinth. My bread crumbs had gone undropped, so how would I find my way out? When did the house end? Or did it? Illogical fear gripping me again; I fought to dismiss it. Another crash, louder this one, accompanied by a ripping, rending sound. Then a scream—not a human scream.

Wrench a rusty nail from a board, slam a door, unblock a clogged drain, drag a knife down the length of a pane of glass. Feed these sounds into Hollywood's most powerful audio blender capable of creating the shrieks of dinosaurs. Pipe the new sound through the amplifiers of Dodger Stadium—*that's* the scream I heard.

It surrounded me, as if I were inside the scream. A cry of agony which intensified, bringing me to my knees, snapping my teeth together, rattling my eyes in their sockets as it filled my head and tried to force its way out again.

And then I knew that the house had not been silent: it had been blocking me. It had played me like Second Base. Me: the great magician, Jefferson Taz, outsmarted by lathe and plaster and wood-wrapped evil.

I knelt on the carpet, eyes squeezed tight, fighting the hideous echoing sound in my head. Then, without warning, it faded--no, *drained* away—liquid sound pouring out of my ears. I looked at the palm of my hand, expecting to see a puddle of this liquid sound. But I found skin moistened only by the perspiration of fear.

Then I felt a ripple, as if an army of mice had just moved beneath me, running beneath the carpet. Looking up, I watched that same ripple moving across the walls, across the ceiling—the wood and brick were fluid, a house-shaped pond disturbed by a skipped stone.

A trio of screams--now definitely human--rode on that ripple and merged into one anguished cry. I took off down the corridor, retracing my steps, racing toward the foyer where I'd left Josek and his contractors.

There was no shaking or trembling, no boulders of crumbling sheet rock raining down, no slamming doors to prevent me. The house was not destroying itself. There was just the rippling across the walls and floor and the sick uneasiness in my stomach.

I reached the foyer and saw why the men had screamed.

My eyes found Ed first, closest to the door. The back of his bald head, the muscular back beneath the sweat-stained wife-beater T-shirt, his thick upper thighs—that was all that was visible. The rest of his body disappeared into the wall, his legs vanishing into the solid floor. There was no seam, no bubbling elasticity to give the walls or floor the illusion that they were anything but wood and plaster. Yet there was only thirty percent of Ed in the room. More accurately, seventy percent of Ed was now *in the room.*

Splinters of wood and plaster covered the floor and sheet-draped furniture like architectural gore. I searched the room for signs of life, as Ed was no longer even twitching. I couldn't force my legs to carry me past the threshold of the narrow hallway.

At first, I'd overlooked him, but I found what was left of paunchy Isaac. The tips of his work boots protruded from the molding near the floor--not quite touching the all-too-solid hardwood boards which vanished beneath the powder-covered rug. There was nothing left to be seen--save the head of his sledgehammer poking out of the smooth off-white wall, about where waist-height should be.

Then I found Josek. The house was finishing what it had started.

He was near the chair where I'd last seen him. Like Ed, he was half-in, half-out, this time the floor had gotten him. Josek's pain-streaked face stared up at me, his ice-blue eye bulging in agony, his breath coming in hitching rasps through his gaping mouth as the floor constricted his chest. His left hand was disappearing at the wrist, but he flexed the scarred fingers out to me, pleading, mouth forming the words "help me", but the only sound issuing forth was like the hiss of escaping steam.

At that moment, with Josek's begging face filling my vision, the ripple returned—this time it was more like a spasm. It was as if the entire house contracted, the floor leaping away from my feet, sending me crashing into the door frame. Stunned by the sudden movement as well as the sudden pain as my shoulder struck the very solid wood, I slid into the terrible room.

The spasm—the contraction—seemed to stretch the room taught, and I could see the shapes of the men swallowed inside the walls and floor. Isaac's face beneath the plaster was a smooth, raised relief of silent screaming horror, shallow wells for gaping mouth and tormented eyes.

Something else: as the room began to relax, the spasm subsiding, I watched as a network of dark webbing spread across the surface of the room, even as Isaac's frozen face vanished into the unbroken perfection of painted wall. The webbing seemed to course throughout the room, and a darker substance flowed through it. The room had taken on the appearance of a raw and pulsing organ—an exposed heart laid bare by the surgeon's knife—no, a *stomach*, drinking in the men, digesting them.

Trapped in the floor, Josek began to wail.

I heard a rumbling behind me, the noise of a stick dragged along the slats of a picket fence, echoing into the night. I felt my head turn; my eyes saw the shapes moving rapidly down the length of the hall, traveling beneath the very skin of the wall. A hoard of raised, smooth shapes heading towards me, moving in unison down the walls hallway. Silent, screaming faces, hundreds, thousands, just like Isaac's.

Some primal instinct forced my feet to run, and I threw myself, stumbling into the terrible room. I was careful not to step on—or even look at—the agonized face of Josek disappearing into the wood. I hurled myself against the door and it slammed open, the house spitting me into the air, the silent faces right behind me, and Josek's keening wail singing me on my way.

I hit the ground hard, rolled and lay still, pouring rain soaking me through. It suddenly occurred to me that, though I had to traverse that hungry room to escape, the floor never once sucked at my heels, the door had remained solid against my outstretched palm. The house hadn't wanted me. It had only wanted me out.

I didn't feel ashamed or guilty in the slightest. The house got what it wanted. And Josek received his inheritance—if the silent faces made of paint and plaster were any indication of what that inheritance might be.

I lay panting on the lawn for sometime, letting the rain wash the terror away, the thunder having long since drowned out Josek's cry. I debated coming back the next day with a can of gasoline, to put the horrible house out of its misery. But then I began to ask myself some serious philosophical questions about the nature of evil, and realized that I didn't have any answers. Ultimately, it wasn't my problem. The business between the family and the structure was done. As far as I was concerned, it was over.

I got to my feet, finally, grass and mud staining my coat, and began the trek towards my car at the bottom of the hill. I glanced back over my shoulder, to look the house in the eye one last time. I wasn't at all surprised to see that the door had closed behind me.

Sittin' 'Round, Feelin' Sorry on a Lost and Lonely Day

They all told him it couldn't be done. Not without help. But he knew no one would help him, so he'd have to do it himself. It took some hard thought, but he finally figured it out. He'd have to cheat a little: lay it on the floor instead of standing it up, as was traditional and almost sacred—no 'almost' about it with some people. But it would be easier lying down, and he wouldn't have to worry about sliding off before the procedure was complete.

He started with the feet. Again, another modification in the design: he'd go through the tops of the feet, rather than through both ankles, as it was actually done. Early on he'd opted for practicality over historical accuracy. Through the tops of the feet was the more popular depiction anyway, the image most people were accustomed to seeing. The left foot was on top of the right, the right arch fitting comfortably spooned inside the left instep. The position was awkward, leaning over his knees to get the proper swing. Even more uncomfortable was reaching around his legs with the left hand, straining to hold the nail straight and steady over the arch.

There was no pre-amble; no savoring of the moment. He got into position and down to business. The nail steady, he brought the hammer down hard in one smooth motion. The pain was immediate, but he'd been ready for it. He focused on the sensation of the iron shaft grating against the bones in his left foot. It reminded him of the sound a metal tent peg made scraping along the sidewalk. As a child, the sound had fascinated him, and he'd do it over and over again, scraping a groove in the cement outside his house until his mother screamed at him to stop, the sound was driving her crazy. Inevitably, the screaming turned into fists...

That was the sound the nail made as it screeched against the small bones in the arch, forcing them apart, cracking them open, as the nail made its way through the instep and into the top of the right. The sound was muffled, wet, as the nail traveled through the right foot, stopping halfway through. Another swing was required, and he delivered the blow without hesitating. If he paused, even for a few seconds to catch his breath, he'd never finish in time. He was surprised at how tired he was, so soon after beginning. The second blow was enough to force the nail into the soft wood beneath his feet. He gave a quick tug, producing surprising agony, and, satisfied that the nail had a firm hold in the wood, he laid back and began on his left hand.

This next step was even more awkward than the first. He had to balance the nail in his palm by cradling his fingers around it, holding it more or less straight and centered, dropping it several times before he found the right position. Doing it like this was difficult, but that was the point, wasn't it? That he do it himself. Not that there was anyone else to turn to, really. She was long gone, he was at the end of his unemployment, and the kids at the coffee shop were really starting to catch on that he was a little too old for their company. So what choice did he have? Besides, doing it alone was the whole point, he reminded himself again. Just him and the cross in the room he used to share with her. He settled the point of the nail in the crease of his palm and brought the hammer down.

Sharp, quick, burning pain, but the nail was in. Gasping for air, he forced himself not to hesitate, but to deliver another blow, to sink in the nail the remaining few inch-fractions, securing it in flesh and bone and wood. Doing it properly, he thought, really meant through the wrist, but again, practicality over perfection. Besides, he reaffirmed, he was lying down. Upright, of course, his weight would tear the soft flesh right off the nail, as there really was nothing for the pin to hold onto in the palm. But he'd said that already…he'd said that already. His mind was beginning to cloud. The pain was worse than he'd imagined, but did it really hurt that bad, all things considered? The blood was a little more than expected, pooling up in the palm, running down over the tops of his feet. His feet were throbbing now, but the hand was still in shock.

With a sigh, he laid back, the hammer slipping from his free hand. Now came the tricky part, the part they said could not be done. And, yeah, it had taken some thought, but he'd had his flash of brilliance, realizing that it was so simple, amazed no one had thought of it before. Brains, willpower, determination, that's all you needed to get a job done. A brief charge of disappointment passed through him at the thought that they'd probably say, later, that he'd cheated. They wouldn't give him his due, even after he'd proved them all wrong. Sour grapes, he decided, then opted to give them the benefit of the doubt. He still proved them all wrong. It *could* be done.

But it would have to be done quickly, and correctly, on the first try. His left hand joined the rhythmic pulsing throb of his feet, and the pain began to course down his arm, into his shoulder. Now, he thought, do it now. Red clouds crept across his eyes.

Positioning his right arm, he raised it straight up, perpendicular with his chest, as if greeting someone with an outstretched hand. 'How do you do?' He took a deep breath, then slammed his hand back against the wood, palm up. And the nail, jutting point-up from the wood like a fang, pierced the back of his hand, slid through the bones, and emerged, barely, through the soft skin of the palm. And it had worked.

He gave a soft, satisfied sigh as he stared at his work. With gentle pressure, he was able to ease his hand further down the length of the iron shaft, knowing that time and gravity would lower it even further, until his right, like the left, would be flush against the wood.

A little ingenuity, he thought to himself, and anything could be accomplished. Maybe it was cheating, driving in the last nail first, through the other side of the cross-beam, impaling the back through the front. But so fucking what? It worked.

"The problem with self-crucifixion," they'd said, with their smug, satisfied grins, prompted by his out-pouring of pain after she'd left, "is that you can never get that last nail in." Over-educated coffee addicts, thinking they knew everything. He showed them.

The blood began to run out of his masterpiece as he turned his contented face to the ceiling, wishing she could be there to see his triumph. His smile turned almost beatific as he drifted off to sleep.

Trapdoor

After re-reading my entries for the past couple of days, I realized that I'd returned to referring to myself in the third person again. When I discovered the passages, with the many 'he's' replacing the 'I's, I felt oddly chilled, and my hands began to shake. I felt violently ill, and almost vomited before Ericka told me to get hold of myself. She slapped me. Only once. As usual, I felt her handling of the situation to be rather harsh. Could I have really been that hysterical? In retrospect, I suppose I must have, jabbering incoherently, gasping like a land-washed fish. I must concentrate harder when I write from now on.

Edward sent me to review the new exhibit that just opened. The artist was a woman named Melissa Samedi, and her centerpiece was supposed to be a very powerful and moving sculpture. Mixed media, the press packet announced. "Utilizing conventional raw materials in unison with contemporary video presentation."

As I read, I became suddenly aware that the press packet was giving me a severe headache. I attributed it to the glare on the glossy paper, or the sickening smell of the ink. Regardless of the cause, I had to run to the bathroom and splash cold water on my face before the migraine would subside.

The new exhibit was called "ARGOS", but the artist herself had nicknamed it "Claptrap", which, she explained in the notes, would beat the critics at their own game. No critics, however, have so far concurred. On the contrary, "Claptrap" is regarded in the art community as quite brilliant. And powerful. That word, in particular, was always used.

I must admit, I was intrigued. I had wanted Ericka to come with me to the gallery, but she had rehearsal. "Art is dying", she said as she put on her coat. I smiled because that could be interpreted in so many ways. In her last play, Ericka died. Acting is art. Dying is art. Art is dying. She always impresses me. Which is why I feel more comfortable in public when she's with me, particularly in crowds. I don't feel so out of place. Or exposed. At receptions, if anyone talks to me, I feel like a deer caught in headlights. Questions run right over me, leaving me mangled and torn at the side of the road. Even friendly conversation batters me. Ericka's much better in social situations.

I'd heard that people have felt hypnotized by this "Claptrap" thing. Mesmerized. Many people have repeatedly gone to view it, because, as they say over and over, "It's never the same twice. Or exactly the same experience for any two people." I try not to get too metaphysical about sculpture. Whenever somebody praises the current "ground-breaking" piece, I usually take their raves with a grain of salt, sometimes an entire salt lick. To be honest, I hate wading through all the art vultures and gallery leeches at these things. The pretense hangs so thick in the room you can't breathe. Listening to them prattle on about art and life, without ever knowing even a shard of what they're talking about. Empty air comes pouring from their mouths, filling the room. Which is fitting, because their audience is never even remotely listening. They're giant, bloated, pus-filled creatures, sipping champagne and acting like it was holy water. Clad all in black, either whales or anatomy skeletons.

At one such gathering, I was admiring *Starry Nights*, the actual Van Gogh which had been touring the country for the past year. It is one of my favorite works, by Van Gogh or any other. It is also one of the few paintings that I would actually describe as breathtaking. As I stepped back to take in its sheer majesty, its beauty, I bumped into a woman so thin and bony she was almost transparent. If it hadn't been for the jewels crusted about her—the rings on fingers delicately clutching a glass of Perrier—I would have sworn she was a refugee from some impoverished country. Impossible to judge her age as she appeared already dead, her hair was dyed black and it hung dank and limp from her round skull, which you could see shining brilliantly through her part—a gash of white in the greasy black sea. Her huge milky grey eyes were set far back in her skull, peering out from the dim hollow sockets, like twin animals in their caves. High cheek bones, skin stretched taut, lips so thin you could see the impressions her teeth made as they pressed from the other side. The rest of her body was just as meatless, all sharp angles, elbows, chin, knuckles. The black dress she wore hung like her hair: lifeless, formless, a floor-length sack.

I apologized instantly for having touched her. She smiled—a hideous motion that stretched the center of her face forward and looked, at worst, grotesque, at best, painful—showing off yellow-stained teeth, and said something denigrating about Van Gogh, a feeble attempt to appear both hip and cynical, coming off as simply arrogant and ignorant. "Nothing new under the sun," she said.

Feeling positively unclean in her presence, fearing that her virulent thoughts would foam out of the skull and settle on my body like a film, I yearned to get away, quickly, without inadvertently inviting her to follow. I wondered how it would feel to slowly grind her skull to powder beneath my heel. To feel the bones crack and eyes pop. Grace eluding me, I backed away from her, smiling, nodding, certain that I was failing miserably to conceal the horror which must be painted on my face in bold strokes. Hoping I would not accidentally stumble into something even more vile in my retreat.

This girl was typical of the majority of the gallery-dwellers I've met. Subterranean creatures, aberrations of black and white, who must surely skulk back into the cracks of the foundation once the doors have finally closed for the night. Sometimes they horrify him so that he feels like cowering in a corner, screaming until they shatter or scurry from the sound. But he manages to hold in the shriek, until he gets home and can contain it no longer. Sometimes Ericka is forced to slap him, repeatedly, until he stops. One slap is rarely enough. And the open hands curl into frustrated, angry fists. Not always.

But I go to the galleries anyway, to admire the artworks and attempt to tune out the incessant prattling of the lost, shambling hordes around me, who come to gawk at their new gods of canvas and clay. I try to stay detached from these sabbats. Of course, I go where Edward sends me. Invariably, the new pieces and exhibits are as vacuous as their creators, certainly as devoid of humanity. And I'm usually successful at keeping the headaches and nausea at a controllable level. If I can find an uninhabited corner, chair or no, I'll usually sit and jot down my notes; if they see you writing, the teeming masses don't usually bother you. Words and phrases are anathema to them, an immortality too terrible for them to bear. When I write, it's like I've drawn a protective circle around me, keeping me safe from the scavenging undead of the art world.

Despite my grumblings, Edward continues to send me to these things. To keep the disinterested informed of the untalented. Edward sends me for a number of reasons, I suppose, but mostly because I'm the only real writer he has. The only one who can string two coherent sentences together, anyway. The rest of the pitiful magazine is trash, full of aimless, unintelligible rantings, and poor Edward knows it. He knows his film critic is a drunken mongoloid, a ham-fisted, thick-tongued evolutionary U-turn who wouldn't recognize entertainment if he ripped it apart with his bare hands. His styles columnist is a senile, bitter gossip monger who thinks that she's Dorothy Parker, but writes like Muhammad Ali. Edward knows this, but that is his millstone

I'm getting off track. I have got to organize my thoughts better.

"Claptrap".

Impossible. It *has* to be seen. It's impossible to describe it. An attempt, in spite of myself:

It was in a room by itself, surrounded on all four sides by six rows of eight seats across. Movie theater seats, which flip down when you stand up. Terribly comfortable.

"Claptrap"/ "ARGOS", was a twelve-foot column of clay, five-feet in diameter. It looked like it had been thrust, still wet and gleaming, into the floor, its base splayed across the room, a mushed pile almost reaching the seats. More accurately, it was if a large, formless mound of clay had been dropped into the center of the room and the column grew up from it, tall and cylindrical.

Set into the column, at irregular and seemingly random intervals and at varying heights, running completely around it, were large, square wooden boxes, the flat, highly-polished sides facing the audience. They were hinged: some at the side, some in the center like shutters. And it stood, a slick grey tower, dotted with cubes, looming over the mortals in the room.

I took my seat directly opposite the doors, which quickly closed once the room had been filled to its capacity. The lights dimmed and ARGOS began to speak.

As the room became black, the inside of a single box, high above the floor, began to glow with a cold video blue, which spilled out in thin shafts through the seams of the lids. Soon, several of the other boxes began to follow suit. Suddenly, with a startling fury, the first lid flew open, striking the wooden side with a loud *crack*, revealing a monitor, and the harsh, unexpected light hurt my eyes. On the monitor was a close-up of a woman's face. She had dark hair and dark eyes, attractive but in an unconventional way. She was looking to her right, slightly past me, it seemed. "Fuck you, Veridian!" she spat, and the door swung shut, hiding her away once again.

The room returned to darkness, lit only by the thin fingers of blue light knifing out through the seams.

Beat.

A second door on a second box, lower on the column, almost to the floor, opened reveal a man's face, looking left. His close-up wasn't as extreme, his whole head fit in the frame. He was completely bald, his face bruised, his nose crooked. He appeared sad and hurt.

A third door—this time a pair—sprung open from the middle. Again, the woman, in medium shot. Her anger increased and she turned around, her back to the audience, and, in effect, the man. The man's hurt deepened. He brow furrowed as his own anger seeped out. His mouth opened—

—Both doors clapped shut.

In the center, shutters covering the largest box, split apart, revealing both the man and the woman, the room shot from above. She with her back to him, he reaching an arm out to her. She wore a thin, pale blue kimono, an intricate design in gold on its back. He was clad in a sleeveless white t-shirt, khaki pants. Blood had stained the front of the shirt at the neck.

" 'Manda," he said, his voice a hoarse whisper, small and sad. She took a step forward, further away from him.

Two claps, above and below, and their faces revealed again in close up, bracketing the long shot in the center. Both faces wore masks of pain and resentment.

Another clap and high above the others, a monitor showed the pair in a field, naked, laughing, the gold glow of sunlight and dandelions contrasting violently with the harsh, cold blues and greens below.

A clap and the field was covered, replaced quickly by another image, further down the column: the man, grimacing, teeth bared in rage as he held another man by the throat. The bald man—John Veridian, I learned later—held his fist cocked beside his head, fighting himself for control. The id won and John's fist bulleted out, punching from the shoulder, his weight behind the blow, smashing in the other man's nose. Blood squirted and teeth flew. John began pounding the man's face, again and again. I could feel each punch connect solidly, wetly, hearing the air split as his fist flew; the camera never looked away, the scene did not looked faked in any way.

And as the carnage continued, in the center, the man and the woman stood stock still, on the single monitors, in close up, they reacted internally to the violence, remembering, each conveying their own pain. Above them, John continued to beat the man until he dropped back, lost from John's grip, disappearing from view. John lunged forward, most of his body disappearing, except for the dripping crimson fist pounding in and out of frame.

All the doors closed.

The room returned once again to blackness as the blue lights slowly faded, afterimages of the couple lingered on my retinas. The lights came up.

Puzzled, polite applause began hesitantly in the back of the room, as the vultures struggled to understand what they'd seen, while others put it out of their minds altogether, dismissing it by instantly proclaiming "Brilliant!", "Powerful!" They called Samedi's name. While I sat stunned, unable to move. I couldn't think, I could scarcely breathe, having forgotten the correct procedure, my breaths came out as ragged gasps. My hair and fingertips felt electrified.

And Melissa Samedi stepped into the room, smiling politely, standing near her creation; she put out a hand, caressed ARGOS' side as she accepted her accolade. She was a striking woman. Dark hair and dark almond-shaped eyes, sculpted features and high cheekbones. Tall, lithe. My eyes lingered first on her face, then traveled about her body. Her green silk blouse tucked carelessly into leather pants, which accentuated her legs and hips. Thigh-high boots swallowed much of her legs. The crowd of leeches swarmed around her, burying her, swallowing her whole as they washed her from the room. I had a mental image of them absorbing her delicate flesh from the bones, leaving bleached white skeleton to collapse, chattering, across the terrazzo floor.

Soon I was alone, staring stock still at the many-eyed column, transfixed. Transformed. He felt it call to him, promising truths revealed. My hand was shaking in my lap, I was sweating profusely, my clothes were sopping. Standing, he was about to leave, but couldn't tear his eyes away. My legs moved independent of my will, and I was standing before it. Before the grey-black clay, before its many wooden, polished, finished cabinets. Gold hinged. My arm went out to it, to touch it glistening surface. I wondered, as my arm made the journey, traveling through the infinite space between himself and the ARGOS, what would it feel like? Would it be cool and damp? Hard like marble. What would it feel like to touch a god? He imagined that ARGOS was cool and wet, and soft. Soothing. That he could sink into its base, that it would envelope and swallow him. Keep him safe.

Ultimately, my will returned to me, and I quickly found the ability to control my movements once again. The spell had broken; my hand fell short of ARGOS. I cleared my throat, glancing around, fearing that my sudden bout of somnambulism had been observed. But the throng had no use for me. I was unworthy of observation. The only one who could have watched was ARGOS, and its eyes were all closed tight. I commanded my body to remove me, without argument, from the room.

I left ARGOS behind, to stand silent and vigilant, and very much alone in its arena. I strode purposefully through the glass doors, abandoning Samedi to her crowd of adoring piranha. Outside, the air was crisp and cold. I could breathe again at last. I felt hot, my face flushed, I was suddenly aware, as I walked to my car, that I was sobbing.

The article eluded me. I put off writing it for several days, avoiding work and Edward by telling him I was ill. In a way I was. Not nauseous as I usually was, nor was I plagued with migraines for a change, but my hands would shake uncontrollably without warning. I would find myself crying without being aware that I was doing so. Ericka caught me sobbing twice and both times she'd been completely unable to hide her displeasure. Aspirin was necessary after my second encounter. I completely understood her frustration.

Attempting to write several times while she was at work, I never got any further than a couple of sentences before I was back staring into space. I had too many questions. I needed to know more about the man and the woman. About the unfortunate third man. Had she been caught taking a lover and the punishment inflicted was John's revenge? Was the third man a prowler? A blackmailer.

By the end of the week I was back in the gallery.

I was thankfully alone in my row. The auditorium was less crowded this time, the novelty having had worn off slightly in a week. New must-sees had come in and the leeches were covering those. Melissa Samedi was also absent.

Settling into my chair, pad in hand, pen poised over it, the lights dimmed and ARGOS began it's spell.

With a crack, the first cabinet opened, high above the audience. It was the bald man, John, his face and arms dripping with blood, he was pounding at the unseen third man, or so I surmised. The door clapped shut, hiding his violence away.

Nothing happened for almost half a minute. We sat in the darkened room as ARGOS stood over us, its closed eyes unable to completely hide the light behind the lids. Suddenly there was sound, but unlike the one's I'd been expecting. Rather than loud cracks, there came loud, primal yells, hoarse, frustrated shouts, more like groans increased in volume. Then the woman's voice: "Stop it! John, stop it! You're killing him!"

"Fuck you! Fuck you!" came the man's voice.

Silence. The sound stopped as quickly as it had begun.

A clap. A monitor to my right revealed John, kneeling on the floor, alone, pounding his fist against the bare wood. The blood flying was his own, spurting from his lacerated fist. A second clap, to my left, on the monitor, stood the woman in medium shot, waist-up, standing, her arms crossed, her face a mask of disgust.

"Are you through, John? Are you through being an asshole yet?" Her tone was mocking. It struck a familiar chord in my mind and my stomach lurched.

A third clap and now three monitors stood illuminated. John's face in close up, moving in conjunction with the first image of John in long shot—the movements matching so closely it seemed as if time were being duplicated from different angles. John's face went from enraged to bewildered as he looked up at her, then down at the floor. A fourth clap and there was John's bloody hand in close up, the knuckles split, dripping into a puddle on the wooden floor beneath him. He looked up at her once again, frightened and pleading.

" . . . Amanda?" His voice was soft. Her disgust deepened. ". . . Amanda!" It was a plea.

She turned away from him. He reached for her back.

Three claps and the room's light was cut drastically. Only the close up of John's hand remained, bloody but reaching, clutching at air.

The shutters of the center monitor flung themselves open as John's hand grasped at nothing above it. Amanda and John in bed together, holding each other, naked and smiling. "Love me?" John said, looking down at her. She looked up, returning his smile. "Always will."

"No matter how crazy I get?" He asked, without fear of the answer.

"No matter how crazy *I* get." She countered. And they kissed, putting their souls into it.

Clap. Clap. Darkness.

Far away, the phone was ringing. Again. I should have taken it off the hook, but Ericka might have missed some audition tips, so I stayed where I was, curled up beneath the covers, and allowed the machine to get it again. Soon I heard Ericka's tinny, recorded command to leave a message, and there was Edward's voice, huffy, flooding the front room for the third time that day. The sound could still reach me where I was; I pulled the blanket over my head and tried with futility to sleep. He was demanding his article, struggling with himself not to scream at my machine as he reminded me of my deadline, asking, almost politely, where the hell I was.

I was sick. Very sick. I hadn't emerged from bed since my third viewing of "ARGOS", almost two days ago. I was running a fever, and any sleep that found me was fitful and terribly short. I couldn't remember when I'd eaten last—yesterday?—or when I'd last gone to the bathroom.

At first, Ericka was sympathetic, but turned frustrated again and stormed off to rehearsal an hour before Edward's first call. She thought I was faking again, or at the very least, exaggerating. My pain felt genuine, especially the nausea that hit me anytime I tried to sit up.

My third visit to ARGOS hadn't built on the tale very much at all. The third man was still unidentified. John and Amanda still stood with their backs to each other. Towards the end of this segment, John's hand swung out, but the lid closed before he connected with Amanda's skull. This session left me bewildered and somewhat betrayed, almost getting the impression that ARGOS was toying with me. Couldn't it see that he was its biggest fan? Melissa Samedi was there that night, but I still haven't spoken to her yet. Always too many leeches around.

Finally, Edward hung up and the apartment was silent again. I tried to go back to sleep. Each time I did, I dreamt about John and Amanda, and the third man, and Melissa Samedi standing over them, a giant pulling the strings of her video puppets. When I'd wake up, my head would hurt so bad I could feel my eyes bulging from their sockets. Melissa Samedi's giant hand was squeezing my temples.

Ericka didn't come home that night. Not a word before she'd left, not a call during the course of the day. She'd left me to die. A voice kept whispering, "They'll send you back. They'll send you back if you keep this up. You'll be all alone, your arms wrapped around you."

Somehow, I found the strength to visit ARGOS one more time.

Except for a young couple, clad all in black, sitting across from me, and a solitary man in a suit to my right, I was alone in the room. ARGOS towered silently above us. The doors closed, the lights dimmed.

Crack! John's face in close up, rage clouding his eyes.

Crack! Below, Amanda and John stand in long shot, her back to him. He glares at her. They are motionless, John in his bloody t-shirt and jeans, Amanda in her robe, open to reveal the powder-blue camisole.

"That was your fucking fault, 'Manda! Don't blame me!"

Amanda offers no reply. He takes one step forward, stretches out his hand, almost touching her. John, in close-up: his expression does not change; rage is still dominant. John in long-shot: his face softens slightly and his fingers reach for her shoulder.

She steps away from him. John in long shot now matches John in close-up.

"I can't stand you," she says, still not looking at him. "You're still a child. Thinking everything's your property."

"I did that for you!"

"I'm supposed to thank you? Forget it. I'm leaving."

Crack! Amanda. In close-up. Again: "I'm leaving." Her face freezes. John's rage finally explodes.

"The hell you are!"

With a sound like fireworks, a dozen boxes open at once, displaying the scene from every conceivable angle. John lunges for Amanda, his hand gripping her shoulder and whirling her around. As she spins towards him, her hand comes up, her tiny fist slamming into the side of his bruised and dented skull. His head whips sideways, then back; his eyes blaze as he slaps her with his free hand. Knocking a lamp from a side table as her momentum carries her forward, Amanda spins around and sprawls face first onto the overstuffed chair. The lamp smashes on the floor, shattering, scattering pieces across the wood. Behind her, John removes his belt, it snakes through the loops of his jeans with the hiss of a ripcord. He loops it around his fist, in close up, in long shot, in the background as Amanda's dazed face fills the foreground. A trickle of blood finds its way past the corner of her mouth, the flesh there already red and starting to bruise from the slap.

"You're not going anywhere," John says as he makes his way towards her, stepping over the destroyed remains of the lamp. "You're staying here with me! You'll be as miserable as I am!" On the final word he brings the belt down hard on the small of her back, the monitor catching the action in brutal closeup. She screams from the blow and John raises his hand once again.

Throughout the session, I sat motionless, awestruck and entirely absorbed. ARGOS was rewarding me for sitting patiently through all the previous sessions. It wasn't the answer I was expecting, however. Eyes darting desperately from one monitor to the next, trying desperately to capture all the action, to process all the information. John whipped her mercilessly on every single screen. Amanda's face was a contorted mask of pain, surprise, fury. The belt lashed down again and again, on her backside, her thighs, her robe had ridden up high on her back during the fall and she was completely exposed to John's onslaught. My breath, like John's, had quickened; my shoulder began to ache as his surely must have. I began to feel his satisfaction. John was in control of his life again. Though it certainly didn't show on screen, that was what he was thinking.

He could not allow her to abandon him. Not when he had given his life for her. Did everything to protect her. He was whipping her into her place once again. It was out of love.

It was all there in the multiple angles. The entire story behind the fragmented moments of time ARGOS had chosen to show in the previous sessions. Now I understood. Melissa Samedi was the courier, the workman; ARGOS was indeed the many-eyed demigod. He was giving us knowledge. Whether the leeches cared to process the information or not, I saw it. I saw it all.

She had abused him time and again, humiliated him every chance she had. Made him feel small, weak. Unworthy of her—or any other—love. He had no self-esteem left, only raw ego. The ego pulled back to reveal the id. She'd been seeing the third man behind his back, laughing at him, the both of them. Naked in each others' arms as he waited alone. Sometimes she wouldn't come home at all. And when she would, her cruelty would well up in her fists and she would lash out at him. Now it was his turn. It was her turn to feel his lash.

Blows continued to rain down on her—at first they'd both counted, as had I, but the count had been lost in the numbers. Her cries had shriveled into snuffled sobs and her tears had washed away some of her cruelty. I could see the love in her face once again. He continued to whip her until every inch of flesh between her backside to her calves was an angry red. Without a word, he stopped whipping her—as suddenly as he had begun. He dropped the belt to the floor and turned his back to her.

There were several tiny snaps as all the lids but three closed and hid the scene away. High up on the pillar, John stood, head bowed, back to the audience. Higher up, the belt lay on the hard-wood floor. Below the center screen: with his stooped-shouldered body in the background, Amanda lay slumped over the chair, sobbing, from the pain, from the guilt. From the hurt in general. Slowly, she forced herself to her feet. In the center: Amanda and John in longshot, the only screen to remain unchanged, the master "eye". With difficulty, Amanda turned and made her way to John, walking stiff-legged, as though sunburnt. With four snaps, all light in the room was diminished, the doors closed before Amanda could complete her journey.

Soon the house-lights came back on, and I blinked from the sudden glare, but that was my only movement. I remained sitting long after the others had gone—I perceived more leaving than there actually were, I believe. I was, I suppose, unable to move.

"What did you think?" came a voice.

I blinked again and was startled to see Melissa Samedi sitting next to me. 'How long had she been there?' he thought.

"W-what?" he stammered, staring into her deep brown eyes.

"I've seen you here half a dozen times now," she said (—had he had that many sessions? Or were her numbers wrong? Or was he forgetting again?). "You must really be getting something out of this? I was just curious." She spoke with a voice that was smoke-raspy, yet lilting at the same time. A gentle, knowing voice.

"Words fail me," I said, feeling detached, as if watching myself answer. (He wanted to take her into his arms, to thank her for the gift.)

"So I see," she said, tapping my blank pad with a slender forefinger. The nails were manicured, but the paint was chipped. They sat in silence for a second. "Aren't you going to ask me if I condone violence against women?" she asked. "Or how I did the effects?"

I shook my head, still feeling cloudy and dazed. Starstruck, almost. "No. It doesn't matter, really. The work stands on its own. The meaning is inherent to anyone who takes the time to try to understand."

A funny smile crept onto her face, and she cocked her head to look at me. "You're a funny kind of art critic," she said.

"Why?" he asked, curious. Not at all sheepish. How unlike him. To have a conversation with a complete stranger. He didn't feel the least bit sick or nervous.

"You don't sound like you're trying to enforce your opinion on me. Or like you'd even try."

"I'm not," he said. "I wouldn't. I think the piece is brilliant. I don't even think I've seen it all."

"You haven't," she said. "No one's seen the whole thing. The computer picks the sequences at random, and the auxiliary scenes as well. I can't even remember what order they're supposed to be in."

"Computer?" he asked in a small, confused boy-voice.

She nodded. "That's all there is. A small CPU behind the master monitor," She pointed, wholly unnecessarily, at the center cube. "Would you like to see it again? A private screening?"

He was still staring at the center cube. "No," he said. "No thank you. I've seen enough for today." Then: "I think I understand now. Thank you." He stood to leave, when some buried part of him remembered his etiquette. It felt foreign, but he extended his hand to her—for a second, he thought he saw a thick leather belt wrapped around the palm—she took it, standing as they exchanged a firm, unmoving grip. "It was nice meeting you," he said, his voice sounding mechanical. "You've done . . . quite a marvelous work."

She smiled. "Thank you, Mr. . . ."

"Goodnight," I said. I could feel her quizzical glance hot on my neck as I left. Her eyes adding to ARGOS'.

Ericka was waiting for me when I got home. "Feeling better?" Her voice was venomous. She sat cross-legged on the couch, reading a magazine, and didn't look up when I came in.

"A little," I said, I was on my guard, mostly out of habit. I tossed my briefcase down onto the counter by the phone. "Where've you been?"

"Rehearsal," she flipped the page violently. The edge in her voice could cut glass.

"All night?"

"I was with healthy people. *Living* people. I forgot what it was like." Her blue eyes found me for the first time since I'd come in; they were on fire, yet cold as ever. I couldn't remember the last time I saw affection in those eyes. Her blonde hair was tied back, away from her oval face. It made her neck look longer, her chest flatter beneath the peach halter top. Her legs and feet were bare.

I didn't say anything, but I felt anger rising. It felt good, almost foreign. I was angry with her and I wasn't afraid of her. That in itself felt strange, yet it was giving me strength. Strength to notice that I wasn't nauseous, my head didn't hurt, my eyes weren't aching. I felt good. Which allowed my anger to grow.

"Who are you fucking?" I demanded, utilizing my newfound anger to give shape to completely foreign cruelty. At the question, Ericka's eyes grew wide and her face flushed.

"What? What did you just say to me?"

"You heard me. I haven't seen you since yesterday. Where'd you stay? Who did you stay with? Tell me you're not in love with me anymore, but don't sneak around my back!" I was actually snarling.

Ericka just stared at me in disbelief, in outrage. "Who the hell do you think you are?" She demanded, throwing the magazine down with a wet snap. She got to her feet. "Fuck you!" She spat. I grabbed her shoulders in what felt to me like an iron grip, causing her eyes to bulge and her mouth to form an "o" of utter disbelief. I pulled her close, our noses almost touching.

"There are going to be some changes around her, Ericka!" I growled through clenched teeth. "No more of your hissy fits! No more storming out when I do something you don't like! And if you ever, *ever* hit me again I'll break both your arms, you got that!" With a rough shake, I let her go. Slackjawed, she stared at me.

Pow! I never saw the punch, just felt the pain as stars erupted before my eyes. I staggered backwards, blinded, holding both palms to the bridge of my nose. Her fist had caught me right between the eyes. I stumbled over what I presume was the edge of the carpet and sprawled backwards, adding new pain as the back of my skull bounced off the floor. But evidently, Ericka decided that it wasn't enough, and she launched a pair of kicks to my ribs which I didn't see either.

"Listen to Mr. Tough Guy all of a sudden! What happened? Did you get a couple of drinks in you? Did some art-slut make you a man tonight?" Straddling my chest, she ripped my hands away from my eyes and leaned in close to my face. For a second, I was afraid that she was going to bite me or something and I struggled to get away. Forgetting how strong she can be, I made no significant distance.

"Look at me! I've put up with a lot of shit from you, but you're not going to treat *me* like that! I was the best thing that ever happened to you, and if you had ever taken the time away from your migraines and stomach aches, you might've realized that! But you're not coming in here and playing Ike Turner and pretending to be a macho man! Forget that! I want you out of here! Tonight! This is *my* apartment! I found it! Your pitiful salary doesn't even keep the lights on! Get up and get out!" She got to her feet and stood over me. I didn't move. "Well?" was punctuated with two more kicks to my side. Another kick rolled me over onto my side. I could feel myself rolling into the fetal position as another kick found my back. "You are so fucking pathetic!!" She screamed and threw herself on me, yanking my hair, clawing and slapping at my face. My hands flew to my head as I tried desperately to protect myself from her attack. In my mind, I saw John and Amanda and the third man, as I constantly had the past three days. As Ericka continued to pummel my head and chest, I wondered again who that third man was. It could have been the pain, but I was struck with the odd notion that *I* was that third man, and I almost laughed, because that meant that Ericka was John. But that was impossible. John was a man; Ericka was a woman. Soft, treacherous, like Amanda. And I was growing stronger, as John had done. This onslaught I was enduring was the worst she had ever doled, and the past was considerable. Until tonight, he'd never stood up to her. He'd never been a man—not a true man, certainly not the equal of this crazed woman. Did he love her? At this point, with the fists raining down, the question was irrelevant, even though the answer was, indeed, yes. (But he wouldn't go back there—he wouldn't let them send him back.)

As a final fist struck a glancing blow off his right eye, as a quartet of claws dug down the side of his face, he got his feet under her and kicked with all his might. The tiny blonde sailed across the room, bouncing off the couch. He was on his feet, ripping off his belt, feeling the leather slide through the loops with a sibilant *ssthwip*. Looping the belt around his hand, he advanced on her. She leapt at him, claws out, teeth bared. Catching her arm he swung her around and pushed her face down over the couch. Following her momentum, he put a knee in the small of her back, pinning her to the couch. With his free hand, he gripped the waistband of her khaki shorts and attempted to rip them down, but they were too tightly fastened. He contented himself to lashing her over the shorts. The belt found flesh at the tops of her thighs and at her lower back where her top had ridden up. She was making enraged, incoherent sounds as he whipped her. Her hands lashed at him in a fury of claws and fists, attempting to hurt him, rather than block the blows. With his arm pumping up and down, the belt landed in all directions, though he tried to center the blows on her backside. He felt like a man. In control for once in his life, as her nails raked across his already bloodied cheek. He caught her flailing arm with his free hand and yanked it up and back towards her shoulder blade. There were a trio of dry snaps and a pop, but he didn't concern himself with such sounds. Nor with the screams that accompanied these dry-twig sounds.

Knowing it was strange, he couldn't help but feel that in doing this, in beating her, he was showing he loved her, letting her know that her abuse would no longer be tolerated. Indeed, until now, he'd never laid a hand on her, but she'd hurt him countless times. Bloodied nose, torn lip, these were things he'd had to constantly conceal on those days he actually went to the office. Frustration, he knew, was at the heart of her violence. But things would be better after this. She'd see.

Absently, he was aware of the sound of something skidding across the floor far behind him, but he paid no attention to it, continuing to punish her. Her arms no longer flailed, she was making quieter sounds, snuffling, sniffling, remorseful sounds. Her head sagged forward, sinking into the plush cushions of the couch. Soon the only sounds to be heard were those of his loving blows striking her clothed bottom and her thighs. Loving discipline, he thought, as he realized that he'd lost the belt, and that his hand was nothing more than a closed fist, and that he was beating her back and the base of her skull. In seconds, he was watching himself beat her, becoming aware of his actions, he landed a final blow between her shoulder blades and allowed the fist to rest there, next to her right arm which had been bent at an impossible angle. Blood had soaked her haltertop at the elbow, and he watched with sickened fascination at the blood dripped from the protruding chalk-white bone.

Stepping away from her, he watched as Ericka sagged forward, slowly sliding off the couch, landing in a heap on the floor, her arm still bent behind her. Her eyelids were half-open, fluttering, and her eyes stared glassily up at the ceiling. Blood trickled from both nostrils, from the right side of her mouth, and from her right ear, matting her straw-colored hair. He stared down at the broken doll at his feet, her bare legs bruised and splayed out in front of her, at her open hand, twitching fingers with the broken, ragged, bloody nails.

He became aware of the stinging in his face, and reached up with tentative fingers which came away wet and red. His left eye was having trouble focusing and it felt swollen, torn. Running his hand through his hair, he felt his ear with detached fascination, wondering what was holding it on as it flopped around nearly bent in half, sticking out from the side of his head. A giggle escaped his lips, and he looked around at the room that was suddenly alien to him. Where was the lamp she'd smashed as she fell? Where was the green overstuffed chair? He'd been wearing jeans, hadn't he? Or had that been the other man? The other man had had hair. Perhaps that's who he was. And if that were the case, who was this blonde woman at his feet? Why had she hurt him so much?

Ericka. The name came to him in a flash of memory. Ericka lay at his feet. And he had hurt her. Hurt her terribly. Something had to be done. But I suddenly couldn't remember what to do when people were hurt. You took them to a building where men in white fixed them. I couldn't remember what that building was. It was a special place. But for the life of me, all I could think of was ARGOS. ARGOS showed me so many things; it could help me help Ericka. Why had I hurt her so much? I wanted her to love me again! I wanted her well again. I was praying that this whole thing was a dream—that none of it had ever happened. Then I remembered that ARGOS could change time around. That's what Melissa had said. It chose events at random. It loved me. It knew me. If I were lucky, I could persuade it to turn back time for me, just this once.

I scooped her into my arms; it was difficult, and it took several tries to stand. She was dead weight, her breath coming in ragged gasps. I don't remember how I got to there, but my arms and chest were aching by the time I got to the gallery. Shouldering open the twin glass doors, I was practically oblivious to the gaping stares and audible gasps from the leeches. It wasn't crowded at that time of night, but there were enough to notice our entrance. Striding purposefully toward ARGOS' throne room, I ignored everyone as I went about my single-minded task.

Feeling oddly calm, I stood in the doorway, cradling Ericka in my aching arms, her eyes had closed during the journey. I don't remember watching them close, just being aware that they had. She was still gulping air and her left arm continued to twitch as I entered the room. Standing before the many-eyed column, I smiled, knowing that somehow, everything was going to be fine. Carefully, I got to my knees and gently laid Ericka at ARGOS' base. I brushed back a loose strand of hair and wiped the blood from her mouth as best I could. In the distance, I could hear faint sirens growing louder. But these sounds were insignificant to me at the moment.

Feeling suddenly exhausted, I decided to sit for a while, at ARGOS' feet. Resting my hand on Ericka's leg, I could almost feel the column call to me. The slick-looking clay at the base was cool and smooth, hard, but became suddenly soft as I lay my head against it. I could feel myself slowly sinking into the cool, comforting clay, feel it welling up around me, cushioning my tired, aching body. My eye had been throbbing, but as the clay bubbled up around me, it soothed my pains. I cradled Ericka as ARGOS cradled us both.

As the men in uniforms rushed into the room, with the leeches surrounding them and Melissa Samedi close behind, he felt safe and comfortable in ARGOS' embrace. And as ARGOS had at the end of each session, he closed his eyes and slept.

The Naked Bones of an Echo

CHAPTER 1

I wasn't aware that Jessie Graves was deceased when she came to me for help. In hindsight, I don't know why I should have been aware of such a thing. I'd never heard of her. She was just a tall, leggy, well-built, flame-haired woman in a black dress—you know, the usual.

This absolutely angelic woman slid into my seldom-so graced office and stood at attention in front of my desk, and my mind went blank. Just a test pattern reading "Please Stand By". Then Miss Omniverse looks down at me with her emerald green eyes, from under lashes that brushed the tip of her nose when she blinked. She wrapped bee-stung lips around this inquiry:

"Are you Jefferson Taz?"

My heart skipped one single beat and went on to duplicate to drum solo from "Wipe Out."

I nodded. What else could I do?

"My name is Jessie Graves," she breathed. There was a natural mint scent on that breath.

"How do you do?" I said, becoming Cary Grant, hoping my voice would convey the smoking-jacket-and-pipe tone I was trying so desperately to project. "Won't you sit down?" I felt as suave as Curly Howard.

She smiled. She sat.

"So, tell me. What seems to be the problem?"

"My problem is a very difficult one to explain." Her voice was so smoky, I thought I was in Pittsburgh.

"Give it a try, I'm a very good listener."

"Yes, I'm sure you are," she said. "Mr. Taz, I'm going to be blunt."

I nodded, so as to let her know that I was still alive. Not breathing very well, but alive.

"I want to hire you for a very special case. I'm told that, due to my unusual situation, you are the only one I can turn to." She paused, taking a deep breath (a little overly dramatic, but what the hell, you know?). "I want you to find my murderer."

And back came the test pattern.

"Pardon me?" I said, as politely as I could. Even I get surprised from time to time.

"Mr. Taz, I assure you that I am very serious. A few days ago—how long ago, exactly, I'm not quite sure—I was murdered in my bed. Whoever killed me stole my body and has not buried it. I want you to find three things for me," she counted the items out on fingers so thin, you could use them to pick locks. "Who killed me, why I was killed, and where my body is. Once you find out these things, I would like you to recover my body and bury it in my family plot at Wildwood Cemetery."

I must've been frowning. You'd've done the same thing in my position. At any rate she looked me right in the eye and got rigor mortis serious.

"Mr. Taz, I can only stray away from my death place for a short period of time. One hour is all they gave me. I'm sure you know the "they" I'm referring to."

"We've met," I said grimly.

"Once you complete the task I will give you a blank check, take it to the medium of your choice—I understand you deal with them frequently—through him or her I will fill it out for you, in any amount you wish. I don't care if my murderers are prosecuted, but I cannot rest until I know who they are. This much I knew without their input."

I stared at her for a good long time. This seemed so unreal—and believe me, when I say that, I mean it. She looked as solid as the desk beneath my elbows. I didn't disbelieve her, exactly, it was just that something seemed to be missing.

"Miss Graves," I began, trying to tie up all the loose end I could see. "I don't mean any disrespect, but you don't seem the type of person who would have heard about me, and I'm not thought of very highly in the afterlife. Would you mind telling me how you found out about my services?"

She sat back and stared back at me.

"Mr. Taz, my father was Benjamin Gulliver."

That explained everything, believe it or not.

"I'm sure you've heard his name before?"

"Once or twice."

Benjamin Gulliver...

She stood up and leaned over my desk. ". . . And, to erase any further doubts from your mind. . ." And then Jessie Graves proved to me that she was an apparition: She stuck her hand into my forehead. A sickening, tingling coldness spread throughout my skull and scalp, like someone had licked my forehead and held it against a piece of frozen chrome. Her hand burnt and scoured my head inside and out. When she withdrew, she left a sticky smear of ectoplasm on my scalp. My flesh felt electrified and clammy at the same time. I also felt nauseous. You know the old saying: Made my skin crawl? Well, that's just what her touch did to me: it made my skin crawl . . . straight up over my head and into a corner to hide.

I jerked away from her, and looked up, wide-eyed, at the woman who was no longer quite as enticing as she had been ten seconds before. She smiled sadly and gazed past me, at the church outside the window.

"I'm sorry I had to do that, Mr. Taz," she didn't look at me as she spoke. Her eyes glistened, disproving the notion that spirits can't cry. "I'm not into parlor tricks to get what I want. And believe it or not, I know exactly how you feel right now." She looked down at my obviously disgruntled expression. "You feel violated and sickened, don't you?"

I nodded feebly, not having gotten back my sense of speech.

"I know that feeling all too well," looking away again. God help me, I didn't want to hear details. With a deep breath she regained her composure and turned her attention back to me. "Do you have a pen?"

Automatically, I held up the one I'd been playing 'rocket' with before she came in.

"Good. Now, uncap it and take down this address."

I did as I was told, obeying like a good little Nazi.

"411 Casper Boulevard."—Ironic, isn't it?—"That's where I died. I assume you'll want to see my bedroom?"

Not so much anymore, I'll admit. "I guess."

"Fine. I'm going there now, though I'm afraid I won't be able to share a taxi with you, since I'm taking my own way."

I returned her smile. My God, if she'd been half as charming in life as she was in death ... "I'll find it."

"Good." She turned to go. At least she wasn't going to dematerialize in my office; I wouldn't have any ectoplasm to clean up. But then she stopped just before the already open door, and looked back at me. "Mr. Taz?" She said in a voice that was so soft and small that something inside me thawed.

"Jefferson," I amended (ya big hearted slob).

She smiled sweetly. "Jefferson. I want to thank you. You're the only one who can help me. The only one who would care. Thank you." She turned and walked out. She was probably right about the latter.

"You're welcome," I whispered.

CHAPTER 2

I haven't been in this business long. I would never have gotten into it in the first place if I hadn't died myself. Yeah, that's right, I'm dead too. At least, part of me is. It's hard to explain, but I might as well give it a shot.

Nether-creatures are drawn to me, and I don't mean that they admire my natural charisma. Demons, ghouls, ghosts, and the miscellaneous Things-That-Go-Bump-In-The-Night, all kinds of things come to me sooner or later. All on account of the Sho-pan, the reason I'm in this business to begin with.

The Sho-pan is this blue jewel that hangs around my neck on a chain. Whatever it's made out of, though, is mystical, and those mystical properties were grafted onto my soul about five years ago by a—I'll call her a "woman" for lack of a better word —named Malhaves (which, by the way, is pronounced mahl-HAH-vayz). I spent a year and a half running from the responsibility that went with it. I'm still not sure why I was picked.

Five years ago I was this crazy, enigmatic Greenwich Village artist. I made some artsy movies, painted some bullshit paintings, sang some treacley ballads and pulled a lot of crazy stunts.

My last one was a doozy. I walked a tightrope stretched between the twin towers of the World Trade Center. Without a permit, I might add, much less a net. I was sixty stories up with high winds blowing around me, wearing this god-awful silver suit my friend A.P. had made for me. It was the death-kick I wanted. To be close enough to death to touch it. That's why I did it. And I fell.

After that, everything gets a little convoluted.

The jet-set Jefferson Taz (nee` Tazlowski) was dead. All the followers of Tazmania lost their god. The twenty-four-year-old Warhol wanna-be hit the ground hard and drove himself two-feet into the pavement.

And the shallow Citizen Taz was replaced by the metaphysically-correct demon hunter. I'm not really sure how. (To make matters stranger, I run into my old friends now and then, and it's like nothing ever happened. Like I'd never died. Like I just had a change of life or something. I just don't have the guts to ask Malhaves what happened.)

I woke up in my own bed exactly four months later. My old brownstone—always teeming with fluff chicks, death chicks, and art mavens—was now deserted. The furniture had been covered, the fridge emptied. Tazmania, both the house and the cult, had been abandoned.

I sat up, naked. Around my neck, on a gold chain, in a gold setting, was a blue jewel the size of an unroasted chestnut. The Sho-pan.

Words kept echoing in my brain. "To remove the Sho-pan means death for you. You must cleanse the Earthly plane of the cancers that have infected your reality. They will be drawn to you by the Sho-pan." Typically cliched horror-movie stuff.

That's when I noticed something blood-red and scaly crouching at the foot of my bed. I screamed, jumped out of bed and cowered in a corner. The thing ran a pink tongue across two rows of needle-sharp teeth and leapt right for me. Without my control, my arms shot out from my sides and extended into a mock-crucifixion position. The demon took a swan-dive straight into me.

Or so I thought. In reality, the Sho-pan acted as a spiritual vacuum cleaner, and sucked it in. It protected me, by imprisoning the demon. That was the purpose of the Sho-pan.

I didn't know this at the time, however; I was convinced the thing was still rattling around inside of me. Shooting out of bed, I rummaged around until found some clothes, dressed as fast as I could and got the hell out of there. I haven't been back to New York since.

About a year later, I found out about Malhaves, the Strangeways path, etc.

Remind me to tell you about those things sometime.

The next day I made my way to 411 Casper Boulevard. The house and street were in a posh uptown neighborhood, and 411 Casper was a beautiful brownstone mansion, with ornate stained-glass windows, an ivy trellis and a big steel gate guarding the whole shop. Neatly-trimmed hedges lined the short walkway to the front door, which, oddly enough, was lying open. As cautious as a flaming gorilla, I entered this beautiful brownstone mansion and stopped dead in the foyer.

The beautiful, well-groomed brownstone mansion was an internal shambles. Furniture overturned, bookshelves toppled, papers everywhere, rug and curtains askew. Whoever did this left no turn unstoned. I was instantly worried.

"Miss Graves?" I called, hoping desperately for an answer.

Now don't think that this is an idiot thing to do. I've dealt with a lot of people in the past who have discovered for themselves that there are plenty of ways to "kill" a ghost.

I called her again, then saw her curvaceous form at the top of the spiral staircase. Midmorning sunlight was shining through her from a window behind her.

"I was wondering when you were going to show up," she said with a tired voice. I suddenly felt like a heel but I wasn't sure why.

"Did you see who did this?"

"Of course. I didn't recognize them, though. Four young men, with shaved heads and leather jackets. Vandals."

"No, I don't think so," I said, crouching down to examine the wreckage. "The damage seems too specific; they were looking for something, they weren't just smash 'n grabbers."

She wasn't inclined to believe me. "One of them spray painted something on the wall up here."

"Where?" I asked, standing up.

"Up here. In the hall."

I took the steps two at a time as was my habit. Made me feel taller somehow. She was right. At the top of the steps, to the left, sloppily sprayed, was a pentagram and an anarchy sign. Star in the circle, capital 'A' in a circle. Occultists *and* punks. They'd even slashed the wall paper, spraying the symbols on the the white wall beneath. They wanted people to know, no mistake about that.

"Well," she asked. "What do you think?"

"They're not artists."

"Thank you, Mr. Taz. That clears up everything."

I glared at her but didn't feel like bitching. Despite myself, I was actually starting to have fun. A new puzzle to solve. A new mystery to unravel. Hell, I could just flip onto the Strangeways path and ask Malhaves who was behind it all, but what sort of detective work was that? All my life I've loved this kind of stuff. I love challenges. Sickening, isn't it?

"Did they say anything while they were here?" I asked, still staring at the symbols.

"Quite a bit, though I'm not sure I could repeat most of it without blushing."

"I mean like dates, names, places? I'm sure I could quote the other stuff."

She shook her head. "Not that I can recall," she suddenly brightened. "Although . . . no. . . No, that was nothing."

"What? Tell me."

"I didn't show myself, you see. I stayed hidden, invisible."

"Well, that's good."

"Yes, but I kept drifting from room to room as they destroyed them. I didn't hear everything. But I heard them saying 'die'-something, and 'master die'-something."

"That's it, huh?"

"They weren't the most articulate of fellows."

This meant absolutely nothing to me whatsoever. I continued to stare at the symbols. Unconsciously, I was playing with my high school class ring, twisting it around, removing it, replacing it. Nervous habit. Something I do when I'm thinking. Finally, I emerged from my stupor and glanced up at Jessie—she was tall even for a ghost. Made my five' five" frame feel absolutely miniscule. "Where's your bedroom?" I asked, a question which would've gotten my face slapped in most planes of reality.

"Up here," she replied and led me up the staircase. As she ascended, I watched her move; if her body had been half as sexy as her spirit . . .

"You said they were wearing leather jackets?"

"Yes."

"Did the jackets have anything on them? Any symbols? Specific colors?"

She thought for a moment. "For the most part, they just had names of what I'm assuming are rock bands. Um, *White Zombie*, I saw, and something called, er, *Nasal Sex*, I believe."

We both giggled over this.

"Ahem. Other than that, there were mostly skulls and swastikas. Oh, um, one of them had a very nice decal of a cobra coiled around a swastika. Does that mean anything to you?"

"Not so far. Anything shaved into their heads?"

"All four had swastikas on the backs of their heads."

I frowned harder. I wasn't as familiar as I should be with the local teen scum.

The bedroom was no worse off than the rest of the house; it too was thoroughly trashed. I could feel the vibrations of several people, but naturally, Jessie's were the strongest. The intruders hadn't been in the room long enough to allow the auras to linger. "Do you have any idea what they might have been looking for?"

"I told you, I wasn't under the impression they were looking for anything at all."

I 'mmmhmmm'ed at this.

"Any clues, Jefferson?"

"Not a one."

I placed my hand on the disheveled bed, with its mattress lying half-on, half-off the frame. The vibrations I felt almost knocked the proverbial wind out of me. Jessie had been murdered alright, but by something . . . not quite right. For some reason, I had the weirdest feeling the murderer wasn't even in the room when he killed her.

Whoever Jessie's killer was, he was powerful, and I wasn't at all sure of what I was dealing with. Rather than fill her with false hopes or fears, I simply nodded and left the room. Jessie didn't say a word, but she definitely looked at me funny. I went into the hall and began to nose around the walls, looking for more clues.

And then I noticed the smell. Just to be sure, I checked the bottoms of both shoes, even though what I was smelling was rotten meat.

"Where's your kitchen?" I asked.

"Hungry?"

"No. "

She led the way. But I knew immediately that the smell wasn't coming from there, so I decided to follow my nose, and it led me right to the source of the smell. I'd walked right past it when I'd first come in. Beneath an overturned chair, tied up in a duffel bag, wrapped up in one of the curtains, was a body. It was male, balding, naked and had had its heart cut out—with a spoon, judging from the raggedness of the wound.

I unwrapped him and almost gagged. He'd been dead for a few days at least. I looked up at Jessie. She didn't look at all well, even taking her own death into consideration.

"Know him?" I asked.

She answered very flatly. "Jasper Melliner. He's my father's attourney. The executor of his will. He would have been the executor of mine as well."

"I think it's time to let the police in on this," I said, and rewrapped poor old Jasper.

CHAPTER 3

It would be just my luck that, of all the cops in the district, Laughlin would be the one to show up. Lt. Henry Q. Laughlin was and is the epitome` of the hard-nosed redneck cop. Just the kind of guy that was always giving us honest P.I.'s a hard time just for the sake of sadism. In a word, he hates me. Even when I send him flowers on his birthday. Okay, so I sign the card: "To Snookie, from Debbie Love-Buns", and his wife beats the hell out of him. Fuck 'im if he can't take a joke.

"Alright, dickhead, I know you're up ta somethin', so give!" Laughlin snarled at me around his ever-present cigar. He chomped the poor lil' thing mercilessly, day in, day out. I wish he'd either swallow it, or light it.

"Hey, Laughlin! Lotta weather we've been havin', huh?" I said with a smile so wide, the corners of my mouth met in the back of my head and shook hands. It was a smile so warm, so sincere, containing not even the slightest hint of "Go Fuck Yourself". I was proud of myself for conjuring up such a smile on such short notice without even thinking of Muppets.

He hates me.

"Look. I'm gonna say this slow so you don't mistake anything I say for a straight line. You are one hundred percent asshole. I hate the sight of you. When I see you, I want to puke."

"Don't hold back, Laughlin. Tell me how you really feel."

The veins were starting to stand out on his forehead. I knew I was getting to him. If he got frustrated enough, he wouldn't want to talk to me anymore, and I just might be able to escape without an explanation whatsoever. On the other hand, I just might leave by way of an ambulance—it could go either way. At this point, any exit was okay by me.

"I could have you run in just for *being* in this neighborhood! I don't even know what's going on yet, but the very fact you of all people called me, leads me to believe that I'm not gonna like it! Keep out of my way! And if you open that big mouth of yours again, I'm gonna ram my fist down your throat! You got that, smart guy?"

Some day, I'm actually gonna learn that when someone tells me to shut up, I should really shut up. Some day. Unfortunately, I hadn't learned it yet. So instead, I antagonized a five-ten, two hundred pound plus, ex-heavyweight boxing, nil sense of humor, cop.

"*Ja wohl, mein herr!*" I said, clicking my heels and standing ramrod straight.

I'm five-five, one-twenty after a big meal, and not as smart as I think I am.

He drew back and kicked me in the balls. I wound up French-kissing the lawn as the world spun out from under my feet in a giant upheaval of the worst pain of my young life. I never claimed to be very bright. Remember that World Trade Center thing I told you about?

He didn't have to laugh, though.

"What do you have to say, now, asshole?" He grinned down at me, like some satanic butcher to a future plate of veal.

I looked up. I really and truly wanted to say, "Let me get back to you on that." But all I could do was cough and beg the powers that be not to give him the satisfaction of seeing me puke. With a last smug smile plastered across his flabby blood-hound lips, he turned away and stalked into the house.

A pair of feminine feet, clad in police issue, black patent leather, size five shoes, appeared before my glazed over eyes. Frankie's silk-soft voice drifted down to my level and hung about my ears like a long-forgotten melody.

"Gee, Taz, nice to see you're still a jerk. At least some things in this world never change."

I managed to push forward with my toes and kiss the top of one shoe.

"Need a hand, o'mighty sorcerer?" she asked.

It took me a second, but I managed to respond. "I got two, but they're sorta wrapped around my balls at the moment."

She reached down and yanked me to my feet by my collar. New pain arrived to keep the old pain company and they both set up house in my groin and stomach area. I was going to spew eventually, this much I knew, and I wasn't going to receive advanced notice.

"So what's the story, Taz?"

"In the beginning, God invented man..."

"Do I have to kick you to get a straight answer?" Her deep brown eyes told me she wasn't amused.

Since I didn't want to spit my testicles out onto the lawn, I immediately stopped joking. It was probably the smartest thing I'd done all day. I looked her directly in the eye. It's a habit I have.

"The corpse in the curtains is a guy named Jasper Melliner. He's an attorney, executor of Benjamin Gulliver's and Jessie Graves' wills. I also have reason to believe Jessie Graves was murdered. Most likely by the same people."

"What makes you think she was murdered?"

I talk too much, you know that?

"Er, well, I couldn't find her body."

Frankie stared at me, not even blinking. "She a client of yours?" She said finally.

"You could say that."

"What'd she hire you to find before she disappeared?"

"Now, Frankie, that's confidential. My office is like a priest's confessional."

"Cut the bullshit, please. You're as close to being a priest as I am to Mother Theresa."

"That was one of our games as I recall."

Frankie didn't even give me the satisfaction of looking annoyed. "Ancient history, Taz. I'm not sixteen anymore."

"Not since May, anyway."

She glared at me and I shut up quick. Hey, I'm learning, I'm learning. I decided to change the subject. "Frankie, where do the local hoods hang out? Punks, you know, Satanists?"

Her expression didn't change. Maybe it's my deodorant. "The YWCA. No? How 'bout The Christian Science Reading Room? Did you try there?"

I was beginning to see why people took such pleasure beating the snot out of me. Sarcasm is extremely frustrating.

"Frankie, I live all the way down town. I wouldn't recognize a local punk if he landed on me."

She sighed and turned to face me and I didn't at all like the way she was looking at me. "Let's trade, Taz. Before Laughlin comes back."

"You know as well as I do that nothing I say is going to cut any ice with Laughing boy, so why bother?"

"You want to know where the punks are. I want to know why you're here. Why'd she hire you?"

" 'Where the punks are?' Sounds like a Sandra Dee movie."

"Fine, suit yourself. Find your own playmates." She shrugged and headed back to her black and white.

"You won't believe me, Frankie. You never do."

"Taz, I know you're into some weird shit. I know. But I have to know what you're doing here. If you don't give me some reasonable explanation, you know as well as I do, Laughlin's gonna have your ass for trespassing or vandalism or any number of things."

The thought of being "interrogated" by Laughlin made my blood chill. "Alright," I said. I was going to go for broke. I walked over to the black and white and told her all I knew in the harshest whisper I could achieve. By the time I was done, I thought she was going to give me a breathalyzer.

"You know," she said with a very serious stare. "When you and that ex-government guy—what was his name? Rhodes—tore apart half that high school last year, I really wanted to believe the story."

"There *were* demons, Frankie!" To my dismay, I found that I was whining. So much for re-establishing my credibility.

"But this actually sounds plausible, y'know? Compared to the other earth-shattering things you say you've been involved in."

"Look, you asked. Now, gimme a hang-out for Satanists."

She clicked her tongue off the back of her front teeth and scratched her cheek with a forefinger.

"Frankie . . ." I was getting tired of this. "You don't want to believe me, fine," I said. "You're the only one I'd trust enough to tell a story like this to. Feel honored, graced or the recipient of bullshit, but things are going to get ugly before they come up roses. I want one hangout."

"Why don't you ask that witch you told me about?"

"Goddamn it! Frankie, I want to work on *this* plane existence! You never *did* understand me."

"You got that right, Taz. I didn't understand you when you were a drugged-up artist and I don't believe you now that you're a refugee from a comic book. I used to love you so I went along with some crazy shit for a long time. But I'm all over that now."

"Yeah. You're better now. Sorry to bother you, Frankie. " I turned away from her big brown eyes without so much as a bow or a tip of my imaginary hat. So much for chivalry.

"The playground." She called from behind me. I turned around.

"Pardon me, m'lady?"

Much to my surprise, Sergeant Francine Gerrard blushed, giving me a brief glimpse of the woman I used to be in love with a thousand me's ago. I used to use that 'm'lady' phrase a lot before I "died", as a term of endearment and chivalry. It slipped out just then, but it felt good to say it again. It was a very private title, once upon a time. She got a hold of herself all too quick.

"Try the playground. It's on Furnace Avenue. Now you better get out of here. Here comes Laughlin."

"Thank you, Frankie." I said, with more meaning then I have done in a long time.

"Leave, Taz. Just go."

The bitterness crossed the distance between us and widened the space. I wanted more than anything to thank her again, but she'd already gotten into her car and driven away.

CHAPTER 4

I felt like shit for more reasons than one. But, ever dutiful, I dragged myself off in the wrong direction to find this playground. I stopped and asked for directions twice and, walking like John Wayne, eventually found this deceitfully pleasant-sounding place.

Furnace Street is in a section of up-town that no self-respecting yuppie would claim as his own. The sort of area that is all but denied by those who inhabit places like Casper Avenue. It's dirty, it smells bad, the streets have potholes, the houses are run down, you'd never think that an area like Furnace Street would even exist in a place like uptown.

    I have no idea what kind of games were played in this playground, but I don't think they were of the preferred organized variety. Broken glass littered the fenced in area, gaping holes spotted the link-fence. It was deserted, as it probably always was at that hour of the morning. Skeletal remains of the swing sets creaked as the barren chains swung in the suddenly icy breeze. Beneath the forgotten see-saws and slides, swallowed up by the dead grass, were painful memories of a piece of land, whose sole purpose in life was to bring pleasure to young children. Like most things in life, its purpose was corrupted.

    I couldn't detect a living soul, but I could feel the playground's memories. Millions of ghosts haunted this place. It saddened me. It really did. Because I know what its like to be used and abandoned. I felt a strange empathy for this playground.

    I squeezed through the padlocked fence and wandered around the dead place, kicking stones and broken bottles as I meandered. I had a feeling that someone was going to show up soon, if not the persons I wanted, then someone who could take me to them.

    Looking up at the sky, I could see dark clouds drifting overhead. Rain was all I needed today. I spotted an enclosed picnic pagoda standing atop a weed-covered hill, not too far from where I entered. Scarred, worn picnic tables and benches stood silent, like the remains of some long extinct animal. I made my way over to the pagoda.

    Etched in chalk upon the cement floor of the enclosure, was a crude pentagram, stubs of candle dotted each of the star's five points. Flies swarmed around the gutted cat, which lay in the center of the symbol. The smell hit me like a hammer, and for the second time today,

I gagged. The cat was a fresh kill, I thought, as I stumbled coughing into the open air; last night at the most.

I dry heaved into the weeds for a moment and that's when I knew I was being watched. How they snuck up on me, I'll never know, but it was their turf, not mine. Their secrets, their rules. Before I could turn, one of them hit me across the neck and across the backs of my knees. I went sprawling into the dirt. I twisted around onto my back, my feet entangling the legs of one of them, and I took one down with me. He hit the ground face first, and I jabbed my elbow into the back of his head.

I looked up quick. There were two of them standing over me, dressed in blue jean jackets, couldn't be more than sixteen or seventeen. I was leaning on another. They were skin heads, or, rather, wanted to be; they sported crew cuts, but their heads weren't really shaved. The shortest of the two was holding a knife, the other, a broken broomstick, which was what got me in the first place.

I rolled on top of the one I'd grounded, and grabbed his wrist, twisting it up into his shoulder-blade. I yanked him up and the two of us soon stood on our feet in one quick movement. I held him like a shield. His buddy with the stick, however, was none too bright, and as I got us standing, he took as swing at my head, bringing the stick squarely across the jaw of his friend.

"Hey, neat trick, pal," I said, as my shield spat blood and teeth into the weeds.

"Who the fuck are you, motherfucker?" Stick said, displaying his remarkable inability to grasp the English language.

"Go home and suck soap, asshole!" I admit it, I was mad.

"This is our turf, fucker! Pay the toll and get the fuck out!"

"You certainly have a way with word," I sighed, then turned my attention to the shorter one. "Hey, you look smarter than your friend there. Why don't you put the knife away and talk to me?"

"What would I have to say to you?" He said, a wee bit suspicious.

"Well, see, I'm looking for somebody. A couple of guys wearing outfits like yours ransacked a house last night."

"The fuck cares?" Stick demanded. Knife was listening. I knew it. Always bet on the short one to be the smart one.

"I do. I'm looking for a guy sporting a snake and swastika on his jacket. And judging from the fact that this guy has a swastika on the back of his head, I'd say you guys know who I'm looking for."

"Owww! Fuck you, ash-ole!" Said my shield, or rather, *slurred* my shield, through a mouthful of broken teeth. I yanked his arm a little harder.

"You be quiet, I'm not talking to you."

His other arm shot back towards my balls. I was still feeling Laughlin's kick from this morning and I wasn't about to let Captain Crew-cut get a hold of them. I grabbed his free hand with my free hand and yanked it back to meet his other. Locking my fist around both of my shield's thumbs, I kept my left hand free, and had no further worries from him.

"Now then," I said to my knew friend, Knife. "Let's talk."

"We don't fuckin' know him!" Stick shouted.

"I'm not talking to you either! So shut up!" I looked at Knife. "What's it gonna be, sport. C'mon, you're smarter than these guys, I can see it. Prove it to me. Help me out here."

"Why should I?" He said, putting on a tough guy attitude.

"Because, I have a gun in my pocket, and I'm about three seconds away from painting the sidewalk with your friend here. Then I'm gonna blow away Stick over there. Decide how valuable your friends are to you."

All three of them went completely white. I didn't have to see my shield's face to know it, either. Knife looked around, not at his friends, but for a way out of this without looking like a pussy. Sometimes I'm pretty good at reading people. Even scum like this.

"L-look, mister," Knife said, with eyes as big as dinner plates. "We didn't take nothin' from that place. We were just. . . you know, messin' around."

"What were you looking for?"

"Nothin', I swear."

"Nothing," I echoed, remembering the dishevelment of Jessie's house. "Bullshit. What were you looking for?" I reached into my pocket. Attached to my key ring is a silver English police whistle. I pressed it against the lining of my pocket, making a perfect "gun". Dinner plate-eyes became serving platters.

"Somethin'. . . just. . . somethin'!"

"I'm not going to ask again." I yanked on my shield's thumbs. He groaned and cursed and tried to stomp on my feet with his motorcycle boots, but I kept out of his range. Hardly following the Geneva rules, I know. But this wasn't war; it was cops and robbers. "Put down the blade." I ordered; I'd forgotten to say that earlier. I yanked on the thumbs again for emphasis.

"Okay, okay!" Knife said, and folded up his weapon. "Throw it to me," I said. Gee, I felt just like Cagney. Knife did as he was told. Stick followed suit and tossed the broom handle into the weeds. Without being told, too; I wondered what other tricks he could do. Then Knife took a deep breath. "Let us go, and I'll come back in a half an hour with Dymas."

"Who?" I said, doing a perfect Woodsy Owl impression. I recovered quickly. "I'm not stupid, and neither are you," I looked around for a minute. "Over by that bench! Go!" They started over towards the bench. I forced Thumbs down on his knees and I squatted to pick up the knife. I shoved it in my pocket. Thumbs tried to squirm out of my grip, but I twisted a little and yanked him to his feet. The two of us joined his friends at the near-by bench.

"This Dymas guy close?" I asked Shorty (which is kind of an unfair thing to call him because he was taller than I am—but then again, who isn't?).

"Yeah, real close."

I nodded to Stick. "Send him. Bring back Dymas only! Anyone else and you're all screwed, got that?"

Shorty nodded to Stick. It looked to me that we were all using too many syllables for poor Stick. So I said, "You go, get Dymas. Nobody else. And no one get dead!" Stick got the point and took off. He vaulted the fence and disappeared down the street.

I turned my attention to Shorty. He didn't even wait for me to ask any questions. "Look, we were just doing like Dymas said. When you meet him, you'll see that we didn't have a choice. He would've killed us, mister." Shorty was playing it smart, so was his buddy, Thumbs, for that matter. It was making me nervous. Shorty looked to be on the verge of tears, though.

Thumbs tried to break free again. I took my free hand out of my pocket and slammed his head on the bench and held it there. "Quit it!" I said, and bounced him again. "Tell him to quit it!" I yelled to Shorty.

"Sike, knock it off!" He growled.

"Hey, fuck the both of you!" Sike yelled. There were tears streaming down his face, which, incidentally, was beet red with frustration and humiliation. "You're dead meat, Shteve, and you know it! Dymash'll kill you! He'll fuckin' kill you! He'll kill you both!"

"Sike," I said, softly. "Shut up!" And I bounced him again, though not as softly. I hated doing things like this, I really did. Believe me.

"Look," I said with a sigh. "Steve? That your name?" Shorty nodded, and I didn't have to think of him as Shorty anymore.

"Look, Steve. I'm not a cop, I'm not going to bust you. But you guys destroyed a woman's house. If this Dymas put you up to this, I'll talk to him. And, Sike, if you keep fighting me, I'm going to put your head through this goddamned table!"

Sike quit struggling after that. Steve was crying freely now, but trying desperately not to. "And then there's a matter of the dead guy, but we'll talk about him later. How old are you, Steve?"

"Fifteen."

Jesus Christ, I hated doing this. I had to keep telling myself that they were criminals, just to keep my heart from softening and letting them go. "I'm not going to let Dymas hurt you, okay?"

He nodded, but I could tell he didn't think there was anything I could do about it. This Dymas guy had them both scared. I wish Jessie had described him better than 'crew-cut and leather jacket'. He sure didn't sound like much to me. Obviously she'd left out a lot.

Then he showed up, with Stick in tow, and I knew she'd left out everything.

Dymas wasn't a who, he was a what, and he certainly hadn't been at the house last night. And he was for damn sure not the kid with the snake on his jacket.

Dymas stood about 6'9" if I'm any judge of height. Even with the sun keeping a minor hold on the day, the shadows still seemed to swallow him up. His skin was blood red, from what I could see, and his eyes glowed like hell-fire coals. Horns surrounded his head, sharp, spiky, more like thorns on a poison rosebush. A tail snaked out from beneath his Bogart trenchcoat. He was thin, but something told me that he wasn't at all frail. With a huge six-clawed hand, he withdrew the ridiculously small cigarette from his tight lips and exhaled pure blue smoke into the air. His aura was familiar too, but I was a little too unnerved to place it at the moment. In fact, I'd have had trouble with my own name just then.

"What is this?" He said, sounding exactly like James Earl Jones. The voice came deep from his thin body—I placed it as somewhere around his kneecaps. Steve leapt up and ran to the creature's side, dropping to his knees and prostrating himself.

"Dymas, I presume?" I said, trying hard not to show any signs of fear, not wanting to give myself away.

"You presume correctly. May I ask why you're abusing one of my wards in such a way?" Definitely a demon; no human gangster would be this polite.

"I'm Jefferson Taz—"

"That is not what I asked."

". . . No, no it isn't." Way to go, moron. "I've got Sike in a hammerlock because he and his friends attacked me."

"You were trespassing on their territory, they have every right to protect themselves."

"That's the way you see it?"

"It is."

"Fine." Two could play this game. I let go of Sike and shoved him towards Dymas and Stick. Sike froze and dropped to his knees, pressing his face to the ground. I almost forgot what I was going to say. "These guys trespassed on someone else's territory, last night."

"A house belonging to a Miss Jessie Graves." Dymas agreed.

"Then you admit it?"

"Of course. I sent them. I imagine they already told you that."

"Uh . . . yeah. They did." He was completely ruining my line of questioning by admitting everything right off the bat like that.

"How are you concerned, Mr. Taz?"

"I work for Miss Graves."

"Are you aware that she is dead?"

"Quite aware."

"I see."

I sat on the table, ready to ward off any attack. "So, going by your own admission that trespassing is wrong, would you care to tell me why you condone your wards' breaking and entering?"

"Because Miss Graves possesses something of mine. Something I am most eager to get back."

"And what would that be?"

"A talisman of sorts."

"Really?"

"Mr. Taz, I am going on the presumption that Jessica Graves' spirit hired you recently, for I have never before sensed your presence. Am I correct in assuming this?"

"Uh..." I said, articulately.

"And, since she has indeed contacted you about the intrusion of my wards upon her household—and she has for you have her scent about you—she must have mentioned the number of young men who entered, correct?"

"Er..."

"Therefore, she must have described the number to be four, and the only one she could identify—for in this day and age, all young people look the same—was a young man with a particular design on his jacket. Am I going to fast for you?"

"Not at all; please continue." Smartass demon. I had absolutely no idea where this was going.

"Aren't you wondering where that fourth young man is? The one with the design of the snake coiled around the swastika?"

"Now that you mention it..."

"I've killed him, Mr. Taz. I killed him this very morning and drank his blood. I devoured his soul, Mr. Taz." I looked around at the ther boys. All three of them were face-down on the ground, shaking like leaves. I grit my teeth and stared the demon in the eye, which hurt, but I wasn't going to give him the satisfaction of looking away.

"Mr. Taz, I was summoned onto this plane over thirty years ago by Benjamin Gulliver, Miss Graves' father. He wanted some-thing that would acquire him great wealth. Greed, Mr. Taz, stole me from my home. I was required to give him what he asked and I had no idea what consequences would occur out of my granting him this boon. I fashioned an amulet out of one of my own bones. I am not a genie to grant wishes at a whim. When I presented the man with the amulet, he released me.

"I then discovered, much to my dismay, that I could not leave this plane. I could not leave without everything with which I'd entered—that meant I needed the amulet to return home. To further my agony, I found that the amulet shielded Gulliver from my wrath. I could not get to him, and he, in turn, could do nothing to me. Not supernaturally.

"Since you are working with and for the late Miss Graves, I am telling you this in hopes that you will be able to acquire the amulet for me. For when Gulliver died, the amulet was lost. I did battle with him mentally, but could not find what I sought. He'd hidden it. When attempting to probe the mind of the young Miss Graves, I killed her—though accidentally. I destroyed her mind. Since I was able to touch her, I knew she did not have the amulet in her immediate possession. That meant she'd hidden it, or knew nothing about it. Her death was not planned, I assure you."

That's when I placed his vibrations. I can be so goddamned dense sometimes. "But it happened anyway, damn you!" I spat.

"Mr. Taz, you are not beyond my touch, yourself."

"I haven't got it either. This is the first I'm hearing about it."

"I'm sure. Are you willing to bargain?"

"Why did you kill the other boy?" I said, not really stalling; I wanted to know, and he'd neglected to tell me during his soliloquy. This was only gradually piecing together.

"Because I needed sustenance to survive on this plane. These boys are devoted to me. They would do anything I ask. I needed his blood at that precise moment. There was no time to command him to find someone for me."

"Is that why you killed Jasper Melliner, too?"

"No, not at all. I killed Jasper Melliner out of frustration. Because he didn't know the whereabouts of the amulet, either. As executor of Gulliver's will, I had assumed he would," Dymas shrugged. "I guess I lost my temper."

"You guess you lost your temper?" I parroted back. I was beginning to lose my grip.

"Find me the amulet, Mr. Taz, and I shall return to you Miss Graves' body—I know her soul cannot rest without it, and I hid it for the sole purpose of luring out one of her champions. She's an extremely intelligent woman. I knew she would find someone to help her. Even in death. Find the amulet for me and I shall leave this plane and never return, I swear it."

"What if I can't get it?"

"Then I shall kill these boys which I sense you care about, and then I shall kill you. And I do not care about the Sho-pan, I can by-pass its powers quite easily, thank you."

"So you do know who I am."

"Of course. What banished demon has not heard of you?"

"You didn't show much indication of that before."

"I do things that suit me at the time. I had a feeling you would show up eventually. In fact I was counting on it. I didn't expect you so soon, I'll admit. Don't look so smug, Mr. Taz, for if I kill you, I shall devour your soul and you shall discover a new meaning for the word "pain." I swear to you."

I wasn't aware I was looking smug.

"I offer no tricks, Mr. Taz. And no reward. And, believe it or not, no threats, I do not want to threaten you into doing my bidding. I simply wish to return home. I have been away too long. Think of it as a partnership."

"Joy. How do I contact you?"

"You don't. I do not want you to return here again. Meet me in warehouse #6 on Lincoln Drive, in three days time, whether you have it or not. If you do, I shall go and you shall have Miss Graves' body. If you do not have it, we can renegotiate if you have genuinely failed out of lack of time. Or you can die if you simply refuse to comply. The choice is yours, Mr. Taz."

The sky went pitch black for a single moment. When light returned, I was alone in the barren playground, left with few answers and a million more questions.

CHAPTER 5

I took a cab back to Jessie's and told her everything that Dymas had told me. Like any normal person dead or alive, she just stared at me like I'd grown a third head. But she didn't seem surprised. Angry was more like it.

The silence was so thick you could've used it for firewood. Finally, Jessie spoke, evenly, quietly; the tone of voice of someone with a firm grip on their emotions. "I'd like to say that I have no idea what this so-called demon is talking about. My father's affairs were his own. He confided nothing to me, and I never asked. We weren't close."

She turned and proceeded up the stairs. I was tired and in pain. It'd been a long day, but it was my turn to speak.

"I wasn't accusing you of anything, Jessie. Dymas himself said you didn't know anything about the amulet. I came to tell you that I knew who killed you; he admitted it, though if it's any consolation, he didn't seem proud of it."

"Be that as it may, the fact remains that I am still dead. His pride, or lack thereof, doesn't change that little fact."

"I'm doing my job, Jessie," I said coldly and through clenched teeth. I was tired, and I didn't know where this hostility was coming from. "I don't like this anymore than you do. I don't know what I'm dealing with here. I've never dealt with anything or anyone like Dymas. He's not your average demon."

"I wouldn't know."

"Yeah, I forgot." I felt beaten. I was going home. "I'll let you know what happens."

"You're going?"

"That's right." I turned around. I could feel her behind me on the steps, wanting to say something, not knowing what to say. I took a step towards the door.

"Jefferson?"

I stopped, but I didn't turn around. I waited.

"When did I die?"

A sigh escaped me and I studied the carpet and my shoe-tops. "I'm not sure, exactly. Three days ago, I think. A little after your friend, Jasper. Yeah, you were Dymas' second personal visit on Monday. I think."

"I see," she said quietly, almost imperceptibly. Then: "Thank you."

I turned towards her slowly. "What kind of relationship did you have with your father, Jessie?"

She seemed startled by the question, and then I knew there was something beneath the surface of this whole thing. "What do you mean?"

"Did you love him, did you hate him? Was he good to you?"

"I—"

"Why do you wince every time his name is mentioned? What is it about him that's so unpleasant?"

She stared at nothing. Remembering or shutting me out? The room was uncomfortably quiet again. It seemed like an eternity before she spoke, and when she did, she didn't look at me at all.

"My father and I were never close. I was closer to my mother. To tell the truth, when I was little, he scared me." She smiled a small, sad smile. "But Benjamin Gulliver loved his science, and he loved his magic. He was laughed at in both circles, fellow scientists, even fellow archaeologists, deplored what they called his "childish hobby", and they dismissed him as placing too much belief in superstition, keeping it alive, you see. Magicians detested his reliance on science. It wasn't proper, they decided. But he was devoted to both, and he was torn apart by them as well.

"My mother died of pneumonia when I was eleven. Benjamin sent me away to live with my mother's sister. He couldn't be bothered with taking care of a child. He assumed I would get in the way, I imagine. My aunt was a good woman, and she had children of her own, older than me, all in their teens. They didn't have time to play with a child.

"I saw him off and on, on holidays and birthdays, but not regularly. He'd forgotten me, I'd assumed, and I built up walls to keep the pain out. Because he was my father and I loved him." She smiled again but remained staring at the banister. "I felt obligated to love him, at least. At any rate, I lost contact with him after a while, it wasn't until I was sixteen that I saw him again. He said that he was going on a trip to South America, to find some relic or spiritual center, I don't recall. He asked me if I'd like to go along." She smiled sadly once again. "I said no.

"The pain had built up, you see? I wanted him to feel as bloody guilty as possible for what he'd put me through. Can you imagine the loss I'd felt? I felt like a burden to everyone. I hated him for putting me in that position. He stayed away for a good two years, when he came back, he was a celebrity, discovering all sorts of interesting things that are now gathering dust in the finest museums in America.

"Now Dr. Gulliver was a rich man, and he wanted to share this gift with his only daughter. I'd taken my mother's last name and refused to change it back. But Benjamin insisted that I move back in with him. My aunt and uncle were old, but they could take care of themselves. They didn't need me, they said, go on, be happy." She laughed a bitter-edged laugh, more of a cough. "Rejected again," she said.

"So, I moved in with my father. I was going to Williams College at the time, paying my own way through a trust fund Benjamin had had the foresight to set up upon my birth. Living at home would relieve part of the financial burden, I saw. So, albeit grudgingly, I moved in.

"I had heard rumors of his shady dealings in the supernatural, but I placed no stock in it. I never confronted him with it, and never muddled in his affairs. Soon he was dead and I inherited everything. And I have gone to great lengths to estrange myself from his world. Ironic, isn't it?

All my life I'd been trying to get out of his shadow and his life, and in the end, it all caught up with me."

She traced a pattern in the wood with her finger. The finger curled into a fist and she slammed it down. "Oh, hell!"

"What is it?"

"My father's sitting room! Where he kept all of his priceless relics! I'd been trying to forget for so long, I actually succeeded!"

"What about it?"

"It's all downstairs! Every piece!"

Downstairs, in a game parlor reserved for guests of the natural world, behind a wet bar, Benjamin Gulliver had built a secret room, reserved for himself and his guests of the supernatural world. It was just how you'd imagine it to look.

Dusty, leatherbound books of forbidden origin lined the shelves. Vials containing various nasty substances were arranged on a rack. Carefully placed cobwebs lined the walls and tables. Miscellaneous objects d'art littered benches: skulls, jewelencrusted daggers, the only things missing were a raven and a coffin in the corner. It was a sorcerer paradise.

"Jesus," I whispered.

"I always knew it was here, he'd never hidden its existence from me," Jessie said, and winced as a long-legged spider scuttled across the nearest table. "But for obvious reasons, I never chose to come down here. What are you looking for?"

She caught me perusing the shelves. "A journal. Something that will make sense of this whole mess."

"Good luck. If he kept one, I've never seen it."

"Oh, there's one here alright. He'd be a fool not to keep one. Magicians like to leave their marks on the Underworld."

Most of the books didn't have titles, due to age or caution. The writers of these books were no fools. They were practitioners of lost and forbidden arts. I soon realized that I wasn't going to find it this way. And since magicians have their own secrets, I wasn't able to detect any specific emanation in the room. Gulliver's vibrations were overwhelming, keeping me from pinpointing anything psychically. I always have trouble with Magician's auras. Don't ask me why.

I reached into my shirt and withdrew the Sho-pan, keeping the presence of mind not to remove it from my neck. Without so much as a glance in Jessie's direction--always keeping a bit of mystery about myself to entice the ladies--I peered through the jewel at the books.

All had a faint glow to them, but only because of their nature. The one I was looking for would have a specific glow. It would match that of the room, for the room itself had a specific bronze emanation, but the Sho-pan was filtering out the unnecessary residues. On the third shelf, a cloth-bound book fourth from the right, made its presence known to me. It glowed brightly: bronze.

Bronze: Benjamin's aura. It pervaded the room because he'd made it his own. The book contained him in his purest form: His words, and very likely his blood. Benjamin was in that book.

I withdrew it from the shelf and took it to a table. "Is that it?" Jessie asked, coming over to the table.

"Near as I can tell without opening it."

"How did—"

"Please, m'lady. Allow me some secrets."

I opened the book and flipped through the pages. The entries were dated and in English. The end of each page was signed "Benjamin Gulliver, *Ghrane*`." The last was probably a title or a magic name, all sorcerers have them. "Bingo," I said.

I skimmed the book right there in the room, cover to cover, took me three hours. Dr. Gulliver had been a very dangerous character occult-wise, when he was alive. Had a lot of dealings with demons and the Triumvirate itself: Lucifer, Beelzebub, and Azazel, the rulers of Hell. Never met them personally, and have no desire to. According to the book, he'd pissed them off on a number of occasions. Thought sure he'd be screwed when he died, but I caught sight of a passage where he explains how he got out of a fiery residence in hell. A by-pass ritual to be performed on his soul on his death-bed—folks, we're talking heavy-duty stuff here.

And I came across his account with Dymas. Nasty stuff, both the summoning and his description of Dymas' being. What made Dymas who he was.

Dymas is a *fuaearsmatter*: namely, a fear eater. A powerful one. Nasty case, too. The only known case of his being summoned was by a bunch circa 1800. The High Priest, whatever you want to call him, faltered, let fear creep into his soul during the summoning and Dymas slaughtered everyone in the room, including a small boy hiding beneath the stairs.

With most summonings, it's general practice to have an unbroken circle chalked onto the floor, thus containing the demon and protecting yourself, etcetera. Only, in this case, you needed complete control of your emotions. Let any fear into your outward conscious, if you lapse in concentration for a split second, you're dead. Circle or armed militia, nothing can save you.

Only in Gulliver's case, he kept control. He made Dymas do what he wanted and destroyed the demon's pride. Gulliver didn't need money, by that time he was rich a thousand times over. He wanted to prove he could do it. And he did. The only drawback was that now, Dymas couldn't get out without the amulet. Gulliver's already dead.

It's been thirty years, Dymas must be pretty weak by now. Dying maybe. One thing was for sure, he was corporate. He's very definitely physical, solid, stuck. I'm not sure that his getting the amulet would make much of a difference. What I mean is, I don't think he can get back now, regardless. He's changed, he's as much a part of this world now, than he ever was part of his plane. The jump might kill him.

I went all the way through the book, but the last entry was made in June 11, 1982. Gulliver died seven days later. Whatever he did with the amulet, he didn't bother to mention it here. I didn't know if there was another journal, and I didn't have the time to look. I was due to meet with Dymas on Sunday. I was going to have to take a different approach to finding this thing, if I was going to find it in time.

One thing was for sure, I noticed this before Jessie drifted upstairs. Yeah, she drifted. She was discorporating. I noticed it this morning when the light shone through her. Another couple of days, she'd be invisible. What's worse, she'd be scattered. Her consciousness would exist throughout the house, but in no definite area. Eventually, burying her wouldn't matter, she'd have to be exorcised. That's death for the dead.

Before I left, I closed the wall panel behind me and called to Jessie. She drifted down the stairs and, as was her habit, stood on the flight above me.

"Jessie, I gotta go. I'm gonna find that amulet, don't worry."

"Did you find what you were looking for?"

"No. No, it wasn't in here."

"Then where are you going? It must be here somewhere."

"I don't think so. Dymas can probably sense when he's near it. So if they haven't found it yet, it isn't here."

"Then, I ask again. Where are you going?"

"To see your father."

CHAPTER 6

A bleary eyed Marshall Marshall opened the door at the wonderful hour of four A.M. to greet his sometimes friend, Jefferson Taz, who'd been leaning heavily on the doorbell to get him vertical. I smiled ear-to-ear and greeted him with a friendly "Hello, Marshall."

He greeted me with a surly, "What the hell do you want?"

"I need you to patch me into the Consciousness, Marsh."

Marshall fumbled with his glasses in order to look at his watch. "Jesus H. Christ, Taz! Its *mour in the forning!*"

Ain't he cute when he's exhausted? "C'mon, Marsh, I don't have time to dick around. Patch me in and go back to bed."

"It's not that simple and you know it!" He yawned so wide his head disappeared. "Buh-uhh-sides, I'm exhausted. I can't do it."

"Never say can't, Marsh, anything's possible."

"Not at four in the morning, it ain't."

"*Especially* at four in the morning. C'mon, let me in, I'll make coffee so strong it'll beat you awake. Then you can patch me in. I'll nose around then be on my way. What'dya say?"

"I say, go to hell and goodnight!"

I stuck my foot in the door before he could close it. "Come on, Marsh, I need you. You're the only psychic up at this hour and I'm in a jam."

"I'm not up, you shithead!"

"Sure you are, your brain doesn't know it yet! Fifty bucks in it for you." I hated to resort to bribery, especially since it came out of my own pocket. Marshall just stared at me.

"You know I get two hundred as a usual fee. Three hundred from the cops."

"Not from me though. This is probably your top offer from me."

He yawned at me, but gave up on trying to shut the door on me. He knew that if he shut me out, I'd just climb in a window and sit on him 'til he did what I wanted him to anyway. No use in fighting. I'm a stubborn bastard.

"Coffee, now!" He commanded. I sidled in and made for the kitchen.

Marshall Marshall was a good guy. Professional psychic, helps the cops out on especially tough cases. But he's not one of those tabloid psychics, and he couldn't care less about predicting Julia Roberts' love life. He has gift and he uses it to the best of his ability. He doesn't advertise. People come to him.

Two cups of my special napalm-ground later, Marsh was wide awake, though still relatively pissed, and sat down on the chair opposite me in the kitchen. He closed his eyes and started to patch me in to the spirit consciousness: where the ghouls are.

I really shouldn't say that, ghouls are spirits, but not all spirits are ghouls. Look up the definition of 'ghoul' and you'll see what I mean.

I closed my eyes and concentrated. I felt my drifting mind link up with Marsh's and we began to resonate together. Soon, I was drifting through the ether, my consciousness on another plane altogether.

It's hard to explain what the spirit plane looks like, because you can't actually see it, not even as deep as Marsh and I were. You're senses aren't used, per se, you more or less feel yourself there. Your mind is somewhere else while your body stays where it is, in my case, sitting in Marsh's kitchen. And when you get there, you can feel . . . what? *Presences*, I guess, is the word, of the spirits around you. But you don't actually see them, you're communicating on a totally different level.

"Okay," Marsh said in my head. "This is as far as I go. I'm pulling out and going back to bed. Close the door on your way out." And I felt Marsh withdraw from my mind, suddenly I was on my own.

I sort of drifted around, repeating the summoning chant I knew, the only one I knew, and some of those Hebrew words are tricky to pronounce, so I needed complete concentration. Spirits came to me with very little reluctance, most of the dead I've ever come in contact with seem to enjoy talking to the living. Reminds them of the past, I suppose.

"Hello? Hello? Benjamin Gulliver, come to me. I seek your assistance."

"Hello?"

"Benjamin Gulliver?" I asked though I knew it wasn't him.

"Um, nope, Xavier Smith."

"Mr. Smith, do you know Benjamin Gulliver?"

"Can't say as I do, sorry. I'll look around for him, though."

"I'd appreciate that, thank you."

I drifted further. I didn't have much to worry about, if I went too deep, one of the spirits would help me out, or Marsh would see that I've been sitting in his kitchen for an awful long time and would figure it out eventually.

"I seek Benjamin Gulliver, hello!" I was getting bored. "Hello?"

"Hello!"

I paused. I wasn't sure if it was him or not. I'd locked on to Gulliver's auric vibrations back at his house, and this aura was familiar, but not exact. Auras can change from one plane to another. But this felt strange, it felt sharp.

"Benjamin Gulliver?"

"Yes, what can I do for you?" The sharpness eased off a little, the heat cooled. I backed off a little. This was unnerving me, for some reason. I wasn't sure what it was exactly that was bothering me, but caution never hurt.

"*Doctor* Gulliver?"

"What is it!?"

The force of the shout actually hurt. Sharp pinpoints of fire blazed momentarily in my mind. "You aren't Gulliver." I said, only half-sure.

"I said I was, you shit! Speak to me! Now!"

It was getting close to me, I knew what it was trying to do. It was trying to get out through me. To leave me stranded here and take my body. I backed away from the voice.

"Come back, worm! You little shit! I am Gulliver! Come back to me!"

"Stop! Get away! Get outta here!" I was shouting back, trying to mimic the voice's force. I don't think I was doing a very good job.

"Come back here!"

"*Stay*!"

There was a third voice, a third presence. I didn't know for sure who it was, but it was saving me, so unless it joined forces with my assailant, I was glad to 'see' it.

"Leave us, Jule, or suffer."

And that, as they say, was that. The being I'd encountered left and I no longer felt its presence or its anger. My head was filled with silence. "Um . . . hello?" I said. The new presence spoke back.

"I am here, Jefferson Taz, I am the one you're looking for."

"Benjamin Gulliver?" I was feeling trepidation with this meeting, seeing as how I hadn't had much luck thus far.

"I am."

"Please forgive me, but I'd like you to prove this."

"Very well. Test me."

"What is your daughter's name?"

"Jessica."

"Her full name."

There was a long, uncomfortable pause. The presence was shifting, I could feel its unease. "Jessica Graves. She took her mother's maiden name as her own. She never wanted any part of me."

"Thank you, sir. I apologize if I offended you."

"Not at all," the presence had brightened, but I still felt a twinge of sadness in this being. "I understand completely. Jule is a very difficult person to deal with."

I smiled inwardly at his use of the word person. "Mr. Gulliver, I am here on your daughter's behalf."

"She sent you? Is she here?"

"No sir, I'm sorry. She's..." There just was no gentle way to say this. "I'm sorry, sir. She's dead."

There was that silence again. Now I knew where Jessie got it. "Did you say dead?"

"Yes, sir. Dymas killed her."

"Dymas? How? How can it be that he...Oh, yes. That's right, I'd forgotten. The amulet. He can't leave the plane without the amulet."

"That's correct, sir. Jessie can't leave the house, either. Dymas has stolen her body."

The silence pervaded again. This time I felt anger tingeing the quiet. "Damn my pride. I could've given it to him. He would've killed me, but Jessie would still be alive."

"These things happen, sir. You know this. There's nothing to be done. She's been dead too long to bring back. Now, Dymas is willing to trade her body for the amulet, but I don't have much time. Jessie's beginning to discorporate."

"Oh, no."

"She'll be trapped in the house unless I find it and fast. Do you have any idea where it is."

"Of course I do. I'm surprised you didn't think of it yourself."

What? "Pardon?"

"Do you think that I don't know who you are, Jefferson Taz? I know you, and I know you've been on the Strangeways Path."

"Yeah, so?"

"Before I died, I gave the amulet to Malhaves. I'm surprised you didn't go to her in the first place."

CHAPTER 7

Alright, so sometimes my pride gets in the way, too. I unplugged from the consciousness easily enough and made a bee-line for Marshall's front door. Of course, I fell on my face half-way out of the kitchen, and Marshall found me five minutes later curled up in a ball on the linoleum.

"Didn't give yourself time to come back fully did you?" He said with that Marshall tone of his. He was absolutely correct, though. I'd perfectly executed the psychic faux pas of "getting up before waking up." He shook his head and made some more coffee, dumping half a cup down my throat so my head would stop pounding. After a minute, the room ceased spinning, and I was able to stand without assistance. I still felt weak, but I'd be alright in a hour or two.

"Sucks the wind outta you, doesn't it?" Marshall said. I grunted and collapsed face-down on his couch. "Now I bet as soon as you leave you're going flip onto the Strangeways, aren't you?"

I glared up at him. He looked like Maynard G. Krebbs with his unruly mop of dirt-brown hair and his stubbly goatee. His bathrobe had red bulls-eyes all over it. A throwback to his Kent State days. "Umph," I said into the cushions.

"You alright, yet? I've got an appointment at eight-thirty."

"What time is it now?"

"What?"

I lifted my head up and spoke into actual air. "I said what time is it now?"

"Quarter to."

"Quarter to what?"

"Eight, genius."

"You telling me I've been plugged in for . . . what, over four hours?"

Marshall gulped his coffee down. "Nope. . . Gah, your coffee's awful."

I sat up and reeled. I took a deep breath to clear my head. "What are you saying, then?"

"I'm saying you went under a little after five A.M. and came out a little after seven P.M. You've been plugged in for fourteen hours."

"Shit."

"Mmmhmm. You know how it is. Time distortion and all that."

I shook my head. It still felt muddy. No wonder I was so out of it. "I knew it was too dark to be morning."

"I got the blinds closed, actually."

I stood up and leaned on Marshall for a minute. He's a strong guy contrary to his physical appearance. He looks about as healthy as a premature baby pigeon. Stiff wind would probably knock him down, if there was any truth in outward appearance. Lotta muscle hidden on his emaciated frame.

"I'm okay," I said, to reassure myself, of course. Marshall was enjoying himself too much to be concerned. "Why didn't you bring me out?"

"I only woke up at three. I figured that you hadn't found what you were looking for. If I'd've brought you out, you'd've torn my head off."

He was probably right.

"Look, I gotta go. Thanks for plugging me in, Marshall."

"What about my fifty bucks."

"You know that was a bribe. I'd never insult you by actually giving it to you."

He held out his palm.

"Insult me."

"Drop by my office tomorrow."

"If you're not there, I'm gonna steal things."

"I know. Just as well, really. I never have the heart to throw anything away."

I stumbled out the door and into the waning daylight.

As soon as I was on the street I stopped and closed my eyes again. I took a deep breath and altered my consciousness the only way I could without assistance. I flipped onto the Strangeways path.

Not everyone can see the Strangeways path, but it's there. Another reality, another consciousness, another plane, whatever you want to call it. You'd never really be sure that it wasn't still Earth, except that everything is just slightly off. Not in ways you can put your finger on, just...odd. As if everything was slightly out of focus and if you squinted your eyes just enough, you'd be able to tell the difference, but only for an instant, and you couldn't say what was wrong. Everything was. . . well, *strange*.

Malhaves' shop is always moving, but the Sho-Pan is like a Geiger counter. It brings the shop to me. And me to it. Oh, hell, we meet halfway.

Usually, the shop stays on one particular strip of the path: Destiny Street. I really, really hate Destiny Street. With its bruise colored shadows, where the time of day is always dusk, nightmares are born, in the back alleys and sewers of broken hopes and shattered dreams. Every one visits Destiny Street at least once in their lives, and no one is ever the same after sipping tea with their pasts.

Eventually, I came across the small, stone townhouse that Malhaves had claimed as her own. A clapboard sign hung over the door. Upon it were two words: Quest's End. Anything ever lost could be found within Malhaves' shop. You only needed to know what you were looking for.

I went through the door. No little bell announced my arrival, nothing buzzed, nothing blinked, but she knew I was there. In the complete darkness of the shop, Malhaves was standing, watching me. I've never seen her face, but I've always heard her voice; since the day of my birth, I've known her voice.

"Good morrow to you, my friend, Jefferson Taz. And what do you seek today?"

Her voice was the sound of dust settling; the sound of a velvet-wrapped hammer striking against a skull; the sound of blood trickling down a stone staircase; the sound of a moonbeam drifting through a window; the sound of an ancient book being reopened after a thousand years; the sound of sound itself.

"I seek something very precious, Malhaves." I had to play her game. The amulet was here, and it was already mine, but first, I had to play the game.

"Indeed. All things in my shop are precious."

To my right, a single light came on from an unknown source. It shown upon a tiny table, covered with a white cloth. In the center of the table was a cork-stopped jar labled, MEMORIES.

"All things in my shop are valuable."

To my left, another light came on, leaving the first to fade. The table here held a wooden box, a gold key, and a matchbook from The Cotton Club.

"Here and there, there and here. All things come to my shop. What do you seek?"

She knew exactly what I wanted, but she wasn't going to offer it to me. I had to play. I had to ask.

"I seek an amulet."

"We have many here. Which one do you want." The whisperthin voice came out of nowhere and encircled my body like a mist.

"It's made from the bones of a demon named Dymas."

"He lost it then, this Dymas?" Dust entered my ears, riding on her question.

"In a way. It was given to a man named Gulliver."

"Did he have travels?" Light came up on a table holding a single book, *Gulliver's Travels*, by Swift. Cute.

"In a way. He is dead now, and Dymas wants his bones back. I was told you have what I seek."

"Always."

Directly in front of me was a table, standing in a new light. On the table was a child's plastic thermos, its colorful sides once depicting Fred Flintstone, were now chipped and faded, dots of red and yellow here and there.

"What is this?" I said. She doesn't cheat and she doesn't steal. She doesn't have to. She does have to answer questions.

"It is a child's thermos."

"Thank you," I said through grit teeth.

"You are quite welcome."

"Is the amulet inside it?"

"Yes, it is."

There was a catch here, somewhere, but I can't see it. I looked the thermos over thoroughly. It was sealed tight. I shook it close to my ear, but heard nothing. Then I saw it. Painted in black upon the red bottom of the cup sealing the thermos, was a spiral, with a jagged stripe bisecting it. I assumed it was a symbol. A sealing symbol.

"To whom does this symbol belong?"

"The Dymas."

That was it. Only Dymas could open it. Gulliver was up to something. It was a booby trap.

"Is it dangerous?"

"To whom?"

Well, not to me, since I couldn't open it. "To Dymas?"

"The thermos is no danger to him."

"I see." Study that sentence Taz. Something's amiss.

"Jefferson Taz, that token will cost you."

Here it comes. Haggling time.

"How much?"

"One song."

"Which one?"

"I choose."

A cold wind passed, and something was taken from my memory. I felt its loss. She'd taken what she'd charged. One song that I'd heard sometime in my life was gone, as well as the memory of ever hearing it. As well as any emotion felt upon hearing the song. As well as any special time in my life in which that song took part. I'd no doubt hear the song again sometime in the future, of course, but my life with that song was now gone. In order to get it back, I'd have to come back to the shop and buy it back, for an even stranger price.

I grit my teeth and spat onto the floor. The witch left a bad taste in my mind. "Thank you, Jefferson Taz. Please come again."

I didn't want to do it. I wanted to get out of there as fast as my feet would take me. But I had one last question.

"Malhaves? Does Dymas have any weaknesses?"

"Of course he does."

God, I hate her. "What are they?" I asked between clenched teeth.

"Ask the sea."

I repeated that riddle under my breath. She didn't often engage in riddles, only when direct answers were disallowed—like when asking about demons. (Don't ask me, I don't make the rules). There was something specific in that answer. I opted to figure it out in friendlier surroundings.

"Thank you, Jefferson Taz," she repeated, her voice everywhere and nowhere. "Please, come again."

I heard the sound of ancient birds flying away from the voice. And I knew as well as she did, that I'd be back. Everyone comes back.

I flipped as soon as I left the shop. The Strangeways path always ends where it begins, and I found myself in front of Marshall's house. My nose was bleeding freely, one of the side effects of flipping back and forth. I pulled a handkerchief out of my pocket and held it under my nose. Then I looked at my watch. Beside the time was the date. I looked at the sky and saw just how dark it was; I cursed and rushed back to Marshall's house. I barged into his house and grabbed his phone, to call a cab, to get the hell out of there and to warehouse #6.

The time was 8:53.

The day was Sunday.

CHAPTER 8

Warehouse # 6 looked exactly the way you'd expect it to. It was dark, it smelled of mildew and memories. A side-door was ajar. I took it as a hint and entered cautiously. A single bulb was burning inside, the poor illumination did little to cut through the inky blackness. As soon as my left foot cleared the doorway, I felt the cold barrel of the .38 behind my ear.

"Move and you die!" A voice hissed from behind the gun. The command was shaky, the person was nervous. Nervous gun-men are never fun to deal with.

"I'm the epitome` of rigor mortis," I said. My assailant didn't answer. Too many syllables, I guessed.

A deep, attention getting voice emanated from the gloom beyond the single bulb. "Mr. Taz, have you brought the prize?"

"I got it. It's all wrapped up and waiting just for you. You got the body?"

"I do."

"Then call off your monkey and let's do business." I squinted into the shadows, but I couldn't make out a single shape. Not even of the gunsel two feet away from me.

"Sike."

The single word was enough for my assailant to twitch. He lowered his piece, flicking my ear with the barrel as he did so. An attempt to be cute and threatening at the same time. If it had been anyone else but my former playground shield, it might have worked.

"Shall we trade now?" Dymas asked, and at that moment, the rest of the lights came on, brightening the warehouse, but not the situation.

I was surrounded by skin heads, all of them holding guns or knives or other such fun weapons. The objects were all pointed at me. I counted up to eleven boys before I lost count. They were all edgy; boys trying to be men.

Dymas stepped out of the gloom between two stacks of shipping crates. He was flanked on either side by skinheads.

In the center of the room was a small oblong wooden crate, just the right size to store a body in. Dymas and his bodyguards walked over and stood behind it. With a single wave of his six-fingered claw, Dymas both beckoned for me to approach and for the other skins to clear a path. No one lowered their weapons. I didn't have so much as a rock. If this got ugly, I was yesterday's news.

I gathered up some wholesale courage and strode over to the crate like it was a grocery store counter. I stood before Dymas and looked straight into his coal-red eyes—and instantly wished I hadn't. My head began to pound and split. I ignored the pain, removed the child's thermos from my pocket and held it in front of him to see. Before he could ask, I slammed it down on the counter. It didn't make much of an echo in the near-empty building.

"What is this?" Dymas asked, with more than a tinge of suspicion on his voice. His flunkies leaned in, ready to carve me up if I so much as blinked funny.

"Look at the top. That's your symbol, isn't it?"

A six-fingered claw encircled the container. It looked tiny in that other-worldly hand. Dymas held it up to the light and peered at the red cup. "Yes," he said after studying so long, you'd think there'd be a test later. "Yes, this is mine. I haven't seen it for so long . . ."

"Get wistful later. That belongs to you, you're the only one who can open it. If I'm not mistaken, this crate contains Jessie's body. I'm gonna dolly it outta here and call a cab. See you around." My courage was unjustified and mostly bluff--all right, entirely bluff. I wanted out of there and fast. I started toward the hand-cart leaning against a stack of crates, Dymas' little army blocked my path.

"Mr. Taz? You wouldn't try to trick me, would you?"

"Not even under normal circumstances. We made a deal. I'm assuming that you kept your half of the bargain. I kept mine."

"You'll be wanting to inspect the contents of the crate then?"

I was so nervous, that hadn't even occurred to me.

"Uh, yeah. Right. Open it up."

A tiny dude with a crowbar materialized at my side and pried open the lid. There she was, inside, lying on a mound of shipping straw: Jessie Graves. She looked rather peaceful. At least she hadn't died in pain.

I glanced up at Dymas. He was staring at the thermos. After half a minute, he noticed I was still there, and turned his attention my way. "Everything is in order, then?"

"Seems to be. I guess I'll be on my way, unless there is any further business to attend to. You want a receipt or anything?"

A low chuckle escaped Dymas throat. "No, no. That will be all." He paused. Something was bothering him. But he shrugged it off and held out his hand, or claw, or whatever you want to call it. I almost didn't accept it. "Thank you, Mr. Taz. You've been most honorable. I want you to know that nothing was done out of malice. I only wish to return to my home."

A *fuaearsmatter* with a conscience. For some reason, I believed him.

"Have a happy journey," I said, and much to my surprise, I meant it. I turned again, and attempted to go for the hand cart. The bully-boys actually let me through this time. I recognized the boy nearest the cart. It was Steve. He was grinning. Looked like the nightmare was finally over.

Until it occurred to me what Malhaves meant about "ask the sea". Sometimes I wish my brain was as quick as my mouth. I turned and realized too late what Dymas' weakness was. The thermos must contain seawater.

The unholy scream behind me told me I was correct, but late. I spun around. The bully-boys were shrinking away from their shrieking lord and master. Dymas had dropped the now-empty thermos and it was rolling crazily in tight circles. His right claw was clutching his left, which was smoldering, engulfed in an almost transparent blue flame— the flesh slowly disappearing as the flame climbed his arm to the elbow. Thick blue-black smoke rose from his charring flesh and invaded the air. Tiny pin-pricks of blackening, burning flesh, pockmarked his bare chest and face.

At Dymas' feet, lying in a pool of water, was the amulet. The center jewel was pitch black, it was surrounded by tarnished metal and blackened bone, hanging on a chain. Without being told, I knew the seawater had poisoned the bones as well. It was useless to the demon now. He'd never get back.

Dymas lifted his head and screamed at the ceiling. Wood and plaster exploded outward, tearing a hole in the roof of warehouse # 6. The skinheads were huddling against one another for protection, too scared to run.

"*No!*" Dymas roared. "Please, no!" His voice settled into a hoarse whisper and he collapsed across the crate containing Jessie's body. The flesh was melting from his face and body where the water had touched him. "I've been betrayed," he whispered. Hope he didn't think I did it. Of course, I was paralyzed too, imitating the skin heads.

Dymas breath was coming in ragged gasps. He was dying. I could see it. He let his head fall and rest against the ruined stump of his left arm. A slow moan began deep in his throat. It began to grow in intensity. The moan exploded as a shout, a scream that shook the building.

It was as if a giant tidal wave of sound had been unleashed. The force of the noise blew down stacks of crates, burying boys beneath.

Other skins flew backwards, careening off the walls and each another. The sound hit me full in the chest and blew me off my feet. I slammed into the wall of crates behind me and slid across the room.

Dust and debris settled once Dymas ceased to scream. This shriek was just a preamble, a prologue, a taste of what came next.

The second howl dwarfed the first. The shockwave of sound caught the boys directly in front of him—and literally tore them apart.

I was behind Dymas. Fallen crates shielded me from the full force of the blast. I was merely pushed against the farthest wall, like driftwood swept along by the tide. On top of one of the sliding crates was the boy, Steve. His head was only barely attached to his shoulders.

When the scream had ended, when Dymas' sorrow had become too great to even howl against a god that was not his own, the building settled, and ceased to quake. I got shakily to my feet, and unwillingly viewed the carnage that surrounded me. The floor was covered with a lake of blood, and Dymas lay in the center of it, weeping.

I made my way over to him, picking my way through splintered wood and human remains. I knelt beside the once mighty demon and touched his shoulder. He twitched, but did not shy from my touch. After a moment, he looked at me, his eyes no longer burning with inner fire.

"I have died," he said.

Any apology would be meaningless. There was no comfort. I should have foreseen Gulliver's trap, his final insult of selfish pride.

There was only one thing left to do. He could not go home, and he could not die, not here. Not away from home. Rather than let him live in torment a moment longer, I gave him the solution.

After he was gone, his soul placed in the infinite confines of the Sho-pan, a tiny dimension hanging from a chain around my neck, I set to work sifting through the refuse to find Jessie's body. I found her in the corner, beneath the splintered remains of the crate. I cleaned her off as best I could. She'd been wrapped in a sheet prior to being placed in the crate. I wrapped her a little tighter, covered her face, and moved her out of the building, away from the carnage.

As I left, a tear ran down my cheek. A single tear for Jessie, for the boys so loyal to their master, and for Dymas himself. A single tear was all I had left to shed. And I wiped it away with a vicious sweep of my hand.

CHAPTER 9

The cops went to warehouse # 6 after a phone call had been placed, complaining of a loud party going on, disturbing the peace. Who the party was disturbing, the police didn't know; there was no residential area anywhere near the warehouse district.

Jessie Graves had been found just outside the warehouse. The cops phoned me and notified my of her death. An hour later I was brought down to the station for questioning. I pleaded several dead ends and claimed ignorance of her death. Frankie knew me better, but said nothing.

Early Monday morning, Marshall Marshall and I broke into Jessie's house and sat in her living room. Jessie drifted down when I called. She didn't stand on the steps.

I made the necessary introductions and a strange silence settled over the room, broken after a time, by Jessie.

"Is it over?" She asked.

"You'll be buried inside a week," I said. "I notified your cousins. They'll take care of everything."

"Thank you," she said.

I nodded.

Through Marshall, Jessie made out a check to me for five thousand dollars—it was the most I'd accept. She wanted to pay me more, but I refused. Five thousand was just enough to pay my outstanding bills and provide eating money. I didn't want any more.

After a while, Marshall took off. I stayed to talk to Jessie. There was so much I wanted to say, but I couldn't find the words.

"I wish I could find a villain in this case, but I'm not sure that there is one," she said, after I explained what happened over the past thirty years. "Except maybe my father."

"No sense in condemning him," I said. "Some other power is already doing that."

She nodded. There was nothing left to say.

Except good-bye.

EPILOGUE

I attended Jessie's funeral on Wednesday, I sat way in the back of the church and didn't say a word to anyone. There was nothing to say. The embalmers had done a wonderful job; she looked beautiful. I wish I'd known her when she'd been alive.

After the ceremony, I followed the funeral procession on foot. It was a long walk to Wildwood from St. Anthony's but I kept up pretty well. I got there just in time to watch them lower the casket into the ground. I stayed to watch the groundskeepers fill in the grave. After they left, I went over and placed a single rose on the final resting place of Jessie Graves.

About the Author

Mike Watt is a journalist, screenwriter and independent filmmaker. He has covered horror entertainment and personalities for *Fangoria Magazine, Cinefantastique, Femme Fatales, The Dark Side, Draculina Magazine* and served as the editor for *Sirens of Cinema* for three years. He wrote the screenplays for the Sci-Fi Channel favorite *Dead Men Walking* and G. Cameron Romero's *The Screening*. With his wife, actress/producer/director Amy Lynn Best, he produced the movies *The Resurrection Game, Severe Injuries, A Feast of Flesh, Splatter Movie: The Director's Cut* and the upcoming *Demon Divas and the Lanes of Damnation*. He and Amy live on an abundance of farmland in Waynesburg, PA, with three dogs, four cats and two horses, only some of which sleep in the house with them. For more information, visit his myriad of web homes:

www.mike-watt.net
www.happycloudpictures.com
myspace.com/randommikewatt

And don't miss his irregularly updated blog:
Random Acts of Mike Watt at blogspot.com/randommikewatt

This space reserved for reader notes. Didn't like the ending to one of the stories? Hey, write a new one here:

Made in the USA
Charleston, SC
12 September 2016